KU-352-981

THE BARGAIN

Louella had no intention of marrying Eugene — but that is what she did. Louella loved Clunes, yet love eluded her. Finally she left Eugene for Clunes only to find that she had made a terrible mistake. Life was changing for all of them, and too late she realised that, in leaving her husband's roof, she jeopardised her whole future.

NEATH PORT TALBOT
LIBRARIES

CL	
DATE	PR
LOC	CS

Books by Mary Munro
in the Linford Romance Library:

THE HOTEL BY THE LOCH

MARY MUNRO

THE BARGAIN

Complete and Unabridged

LINFORD
Leicester

PORT TALBOT

First published in Great Britain in 1959 by
Robert Hale Limited
London

First Linford Edition
published March 1991

Copyright © 1959 by Mary Munro
All rights reserved

British Library CIP Data

Munro, Mary *1904* —
The bargain. — Large print ed. —
Rn: Doris Kathleen Howe I. Title
823.914 [F]

ISBN 0–7089–6982–8

Published by
F. A. Thorpe (Publishing) Ltd.
Anstey, Leicestershire
Set by Words & Graphics Ltd.
Anstey, Leicestershire
Printed and bound in Great Britain by
T. J. Press (Padstow) Ltd., Padstow, Cornwall

1

THE two friends faced each other across the length of the small sitting room. The sounds of traffic came clearly through the open window into the quietness between them.

"You've changed; I can't recognise you any more," Claribel whispered.

Louella shrugged, her face secretive and unhappy. "I don't recognise myself — but I'm still me." She had only joined Claribel the previous day in her London flat, and this was their first chance to talk confidentially.

Claribel eyed her searchingly, a thoughtful look on her face. Just why had Louella come to her? She sensed there was more behind the brief confession than she had been told. Louella was tall and slender, with shining black hair, a creamy, smooth skin, clear green eyes with black brows and lashes. It

1

all added up to unusual beauty and Claribel sighed gently. Louella's mother had been Italian, her father English and the combination in this instance had produced a couple of youngsters a little above the average in looks and intelligence. Wain, Louella's brother, might have been her twin, for they were so much alike, but there were actually two years' difference in their ages.

Claribel sighed again, not knowing what to do. Now *she'd* been in London for over two years, and her problems were all well-known ones. Success was already knocking on her door. Claribel Ltd., had been launched in trepidation, but the small firm was flourishing.

"What do you really *do*?" Louella asked curiously.

"Me — I've found my niche, even if it is a little odd. It wouldn't suit you, my pet. If anyone gives a party I'm in the front row — catering for same. I looked the job over from every angle, and plunged in . . . up to the neck. I plan every detail, and supply everything too — cutlery, china, linen, food; nothing that Claribel Ltd. can't do from flowers to drinks. It's fun. Birthdays, weddings, christenings, cocktail parties — the lot."

"Perhaps I could help you. I'm adaptable," Louella suggested tentatively, for Claribel had not been slow to present the difficulties ahead if she meant to stay in London.

"You're different — you're not cut out for this life. You're college-trained and not very domesticated. You've lived your twenty-two years in the country more or less — I don't know what to advise." Claribel was frankly puzzled. "What did you plan to do? You must have had a plan before leaving the north."

"I didn't plan — I just came." Louella's shoulders drooped and she looked discouraged.

Claribel could believe the words to be true, yet they were out of character with what she knew of Louella. The girl had lost her sparkle, her verve for life. "We come from the same village, been friends from the cot, and naturally I'll help you if I can — but I can't do it all."

Louella's green eyes flashed with sudden spirit. "That's not fair. I'm not asking any favours. I can stand on my own feet. I'll manage."

"Look, my love, you'd better be frank with me. You sail in here out of the blue, and while it's none of my business I'd like to know that you're not in any real misery — or danger." Claribel's nice, plain face looked concerned.

Louella picked up a magazine nervously. "You know about Wain . . . "

"Your brother? Yes, he's in a spot of bother, isn't he? Surely that wouldn't account for your own action in coming here?" She lighted a cigarette, watching the girl unobtrusively, seeing her nervousness.

"A spot of bother? Yes, that's how it must seem to others. But it's not his fault. It never was his fault. I wish I could explain." She grew animated as she tried to show her friend where life had started to go wrong for the Ford family.

Would she ever forget the day when Wain joined the other members of the canoe club at the head of the beck? It was warm, sunny, a slight breeze ruffling the water, the sky cloudless. The fields were green and luscious on either side the beck, and there was nothing in the benign landscape to show that this day would end differently than so many others had done.

Wain, young, eager for his first real test, after weeks of striving, had persuaded his father to carry the canoe on top of his car to the beck, and to watch the opening of the race. Louella went along too, envying her brother this absorbing hobby. With a dozen other enthusiasts there was a brave show. Wain's face was happy as he waved them goodbye. Mr. Ford and Louella watched until the last canoe had gone from sight.

It was later, when they all returned home, eagerly discussing Wain's prowess that the trouble began, until it grew into a nightmare.

"Sure there's an element of danger,

but not if you know what you're doing," Wain agreed carelessly. "The worst trouble would be if the canoe turned over and you couldn't get out fast enough."

Their stepmother listened to the conversation. "Where did *you* find fifty pounds with which to buy a canoe, Wain? I'd really like to know."

Wain flushed at the innuendo.

"I didn't say mine cost so much; only some canoes did."

"He bought the parts separately, and they cost fifteen pounds," Louella resented the implication too and rushed to his defence. Sometimes she thought she hated her stepmother, only you never really hated anyone — you couldn't if you went to Church and professed to believe in things.

"Don't quarrel. We've had an interesting day. Leave the boy alone." Mr. Ford longed for peace, and knew how Louella disliked the constant bad temper his wife displayed. His considerable fortune had been lost in unwise speculation, and since that unhappy day his second wife had not allowed him to forget it for a single moment. She was a disappointed woman.

"It's all right for you to close your eyes, but I don't hold with money being spent on useless hobbies. No good can come of it. Look what happened when *you* started to speculate . . . " Mrs. Ford sniffed. "I'd like to know where he got the money."

"You haven't children of your own so you don't understand . . . "

"And you do, Miss?"

"That's enough." Mr. Ford got up heavily, his manner showing depression.

"You're too easy going. I wish I had fifteen pounds to throw about. I have to do the planning and it isn't easy . . . "

Louella felt the familiar nausea as her stepmother whipped up her anger. Whose fault was it that they were in this unenviable position?

Wain rose from his place at the table. He was a gentle boy, fond of the outdoors, often roaming the countryside for hours, bird watching, observing nature. His face was white and pinched with feeling,

7

and deep resentment showed in his eyes.

"I saved the money — most of it. Louella give me five pounds . . . "

"I came by it honestly," Louella added sarcastically.

"Don't take that tone with me, Miss."

"Then let's stop this dreadful wrangling," Mr. Ford said heavily.

"No," Wain's manner showed his hurt. "I'm fed up with all these blasted insinuations."

"So am I."

"Are you going to let them talk to me like this?" Mrs. Ford said.

Wain and Louella left the room; this was the culmination of weeks of uneasy warfare. They would not give her a chance to say more.

"That night Wain left the house without a word to anyone, and we have not seen him since," Louella turned to her friend in distress.

Claribel nodded for she had guessed at the trouble.

"Things went from bad to worse, and

8

I eventually came away too." Louella's eyes were secretive with pain.

"Your father must be a worried man," Claribel suggested for she had known the family in happier days, when there had been no scarcity of money, no need for the endless bickering that had been bred of ill-temper and disappointment.

"He should have done something before it was too late. Are you blaming me, Claribel? Honestly, I tried . . . but it was useless."

"Not blaming anyone. But surely there was more to it than you've told me?" It wouldn't be easy enduring their stepmother's fretful temper. Losing the money too would have repercussions on them all. That was the way it happened in families once the avalanche started.

Louella shrugged. "Yes. I thought you might have seen it in the paper. An old woman in the village — was robbed that night — and assaulted . . . it was pretty ghastly really. But it wasn't Wain's doing. It couldn't have been. It was sheer bad luck that he left that particular night.

Our stepmother — gloated. I'll never forgive her."

"Beastly," Claribel agreed with sympathy.

"He didn't do it — I'm convinced he didn't."

"You needn't try to convince me — I know Wain, too, remember. He was too gentle a boy to do such a thing." The words were comforting. "It just isn't in character. Are you here to try to find him?"

"Yes. I hope we do meet — but I'd have come away in any case. I couldn't bear it any longer."

"Hasn't he written — telephoned — since he left?"

"Not once."

"So the family broke up — just like that," Claribel turned the events over in her mind.

"I quarrelled with Clunes, too . . ." Louella said recklessly.

"Clunes? Since my time surely? Or you don't mean that boy who used to follow you around on Sunday afternoons?" Claribel said.

"Yes. The same one. We — were engaged at Christmas. He has a wonderful voice and is getting well known locally. Well, we disagreed about Wain and I handed back the ring. He believes him to be guilty."

Claribel raised her eyebrows expressively.

"It was like a landslide; everything began to go wrong," Louella brooded. "I had to come away."

"You love Clunes, don't you?"

"Yes, I always will, but I'll never marry him now. He hurt me too much."

"As bad as that?" Claribel was surprised at the bitterness in the girl's voice. "You'll forgive and forget — in time. One does . . . "

"Can't you see how I felt? I couldn't go on knowing what Clunes was thinking. Wain is innocent. I couldn't be more sure if it was myself."

"Then they never traced who really robbed the old lady?"

"No. You know what gossip there always is in the village? Everyone jumped to the same conclusion, and Wain wasn't there to defend himself. I couldn't take any more — so I'm here."

"You've a lot of your mother in you," Claribel was smiling. "Will Wain go to Italy, do you think — your mother's country?"

"He'll not be able to go anywhere, until he saves the fare. He'll have got a job I expect."

"Did Mr. Ford believe he was innocent?"

"I don't know. He just looked — wounded — wouldn't discuss it at all. He should have stood up to that awful woman . . . he should . . . "

"He should," Claribel said dryly. "Well, darling, you can stay here as long as you wish, of course. That goes without saying."

Louella's uncertainty and strain showed briefly in her face, "Thank you. I'll . . . try to get something quickly."

"Take your time. I won't crowd you. Let's see, you must be nearly twenty-two, and Wain would be about twenty." She studied the end of her cigarette to give

Louella time to master her emotion. "You type. You know office routine; you'll soon get fixed up."

"I'll take anything to get started, but I want more than that. I've made up my mind. I want to try modelling. I want to make a lot of money — quickly. I'm through with men — except to use them. I'll climb over them to get to what I want . . ."

"You'll change," Claribel laughed indulgently. "There — that's the expression on your face that I can't recognise. You look — hard, determined, not gentle any more."

Louella gave her a troubled look. "I am changed — you don't know how much yet. I've plans; you'll be surprised." To appease Claribel's growing displeasure she changed the trend of the conversation, and the way she did this was a lesson in itself. Claribel allowed herself to follow the lead given. She was beginning to see just how much Louella had changed from the quiet, country-loving girl she had once known.

"Let's go to that party," Claribel got to her feet finally. "At least we can enjoy ourselves for an hour or two. It should be fun." She was a gay, light-hearted person usually, hiding a tremendous capacity for hard work, behind her honest, plain features. The flat was small but well-furnished and in a good neighbourhood.

The two friends bathed and dressed, chattering easily, determined to put the hint of tragedy where it rightly belonged, in the background.

"Will this dress be suitable?" Louella held out a short evening dress in flame-coloured silk taffeta. With her shining black hair the colour was dramatic. From head to foot she was exquisitely groomed.

Claribel gave a wolf whistle. "You'll not be missed in that." Where had the girl gained her assurance and poise? It was puzzling. "Does the change in you go right through?"

"Right through and out the other side. I'm out for what I can get from life; you don't gain anything unless you are prepared to fight. What I want are money — position — power — travel . . . "

So that was her brave new philosophy, Claribel thought. When they were on their way to the other side of London in a taxi, she said: "Does your father know that you are here with me?"

"Yes, but he won't try to get me back; he knows I've left for good."

The house to which they were invited for the evening, belonged to a friend of Claribel's. She was giving a cocktail party to celebrate her engagement to a promising young interior decorator. Already he was designing the décor for television backgrounds, stage sets, hotels.

"Simon is on his way." Claribel introduced him to Louella when they entered. "What are you doing now, Simon?"

"I did the background for that play they put on last Thursday. Did you see it?" Simon was serious, yet jubilant. A thoroughly nice person on the surface, Louella thought.

Claribel hadn't, but didn't get a chance to say so. She drifted away leaving Louella to talk to Simon's fiancée, Rosemary.

"Isn't he wonderful?" Rosemary asked, laughing. "I'd be so nervous in case anything went wrong, but he never seems to worry. You're Claribel's friend, aren't you — the one she rang up about?"

"Yes. Was it all right to come along at such short notice? I only arrived yesterday." Louella felt the warmth and gaiety enveloping her and some of the chill began to melt from about her heart. She was able to thrust away the stark unhappiness of the former mood.

The luxury of the apartment was to her taste, and she observed everything quietly. The hum of conversation was congenial and exciting. Rosemary was marrying someone who would give her the luxury to which she was accustomed. Some people were born lucky — others not.

She smiled dazzlingly at Rosemary and Simon from time to time, as they stood near her, chatting. If they guessed her thoughts she knew they would have grown silent and constrained.

"I'm absolutely alone — and the future is mine, to do with as I please . . . I won't fail . . . "

"Do you know who is coming tonight?" Rosemary came a step closer. "Apart from dozens of others, I mean. Eugene Charles — Simon roped him in. They met at the studios — and I'm so impressed I can't wait."

"Rosemary venerates authors," Simon chuckled.

"I do — and I'm not moving from here until he's safely introduced," Rosemary took his arm and squeezed it affectionately.

"Eugene Charles — exciting. I've read several of his books. I'd love to meet him." Louella knew now why she had wanted to come to this party so much. It was to meet Eugene Charles. For years his name had been a household word, for he wrote the type of fiction that

17

automatically turned into a film, or so it seemed to Louella.

"Then you shall. He should be flattered," Simon said dryly, glancing at them. "Don't you wish you'd read his books, too, Rosemary?"

"I do — but I have seen two of his films, so that's a talking point. Did he write *Love and Lollipops?*"

"Yes, he did," Louella felt a thrill along her nerves. She stayed near the door, determined not to miss the opportunity that was coming. She knew instantly when he arrived for there was a murmur of sound, then a quietness, as he greeted his hostess. Louella studied him. Tall, thin, but with broad shoulders. His face was brown and hard, his expression guarded. As she studied him further she realised that his face was closed in a curious way, as if he was ready, in spite of his easy, laughing manner, to hold off the invader on his privacy. It was a hard face, she thought again. He was the outdoor type, weatherbeaten, calm, arrogantly male. He was chaffing

Rosemary, making her blush in a most delightful way, while Simon stood by grinning.

Although he must have been aware that the attention of the guests was upon him, he appeared indifferent. Louella glanced at him again, surprised to find his steady, unblinking gaze concentrated on herself. For a moment she was unable to look away, confused by the strange intensity of his regard. Her heart began to beat quickly when she realised that she was under the microscope of Eugene Charles' examination. He was so preoccupied that he did not immediately perceive her discomfort. Indignantly her head came up and her eyes flashed rebelliously. The moments flicked by unsteadily as their gaze held, until with a slight bow he turned aside.

Louella was shaken, and wondered how long that awareness between them had continued. She turned from it, her hands shaking, hoping that no one had noticed. She was puzzled by her own positive reaction, too. She moved sharply from her position, trying to hide the rising agitation. What an odd thing to happen. Perhaps he imagined he had seen her before.

She turned her back on the room, and presently managed to chat to someone nearby. Rosemary approached her, with Eugene Charles in tow. Louella felt a return of the leaping apprehension, but managed to smile pleasantly.

"Louella — Eugene wants to meet you. I've been telling him that you have read all his books."

Louella turned, acknowledging the introduction casually. What else had Rosemary been telling him?

"Isn't it wonderful of her, Eugene?" Rosemary was trying to be tactful.

"It is indeed — if true," he was smiling, his gaze on Louella.

"Of course it isn't true. I only said I'd read some of your books — not *all* of them. The ones you write under your own name I meant, of course." It was a relief to find that her voice came evenly.

Rosemary sighed gently. "How clever of you. I didn't know he wrote under other names."

Simon joined the group. "How many have you written now, Gene?"

"I'm not sure. It was forty-seven the last time my secretary totted up the score, but that's some time ago; she's left me now."

Louella was unable to join naturally in the conversation, but she hoped that her attack of shyness was not apparent to everyone. She responded when appealed to but was not able to advance any ideas of her own. She knew that Eugene was quietly studying her beneath the banter and gaiety of this conversation with his friends.

Rosemary whispered: "He's nice, isn't he? He insisted on meeting you. He's so brilliant that he makes me shiver. Simon doesn't know it yet but I haven't got a brain. I'm hoping he'll never find out either."

Louella laughed. She liked Rosemary very much, and was grateful for her help now when she might have been swamped in the undercurrents.

"I'll send someone with a drink for you. Simon, dear . . . I want you to meet . . . " She drew Simon away with her, leaving Louella and Eugene.

For a moment they faced each other in silence. Louella drew a deep breath of relief. "Well?" Eugene said gently, giving her the lead.

"I've been a fan of yours for years, Mr. Charles. I must have read the first book you wrote. I was twelve and I disagreed violently with every word . . . I don't any longer." She wished she could think of something outstanding to say, but thought seemed paralysed.

He spoke as if her words pleased him however. "You've grown up? One does, you know." His fair hair shone under the brilliant lighting in the room. How handsome he was, she thought inwardly. For the first time she noticed his mouth. His lips were sensitive, finely drawn, belying the hardness of his expression. He was very brown, and against this brownness his eyes were vividly blue. It was a strange face, full of contradictions. Wasn't everyone full of contradictions?

She realised again that he was keeping her under surveillance and pondered the reason. Their glances met and broke away. What had they been discussing? Her shyness must be set aside instantly.

"Yes — one grows up," she murmured.

"You haven't grown up very long? Are you twenty yet?" He spoke with amusement, and Louella knew that he had sensed her youth and unease.

"I'm twenty-two. It's ten years since I read your book. Your backgrounds are always so glamorous and authentic." She named several of his books in rapid succession, thankful that memory did not fail her. She might be young but she would show him that she was not completely ignorant. "I took English literature for two years."

"Do I come into that category?" he asked humbly. She laughed at his tone, realising the innuendo.

"Usually one's friends do not trouble

to read one's books. I am truly flattered, Miss Ford. If my writing entertains then I have succeeded." He stood squarely with his back to the room, engrossed in what she was saying.

She tried not to care that he might be teasing her. "Do you visit every country you describe? I've often wondered. Spain, Mallorca, Italy, America. I'm curious. It must be a wonderful life if you do." She put a hand up to her hair, smoothing it into place, and his vivid eyes followed the movement, making her feel gauche again.

"Know something? No — I don't . . . or didn't. You mention my earlier novels, when I did most of my travelling in the public library. Nowadays I do get abroad quite a bit."

"You can get an allowance off your income tax for that sort of thing," she said vaguely. "I read it somewhere."

He was amused by her earnestness. "I leave most of that to my accountants, but I'll look into it tomorrow." He accepted a couple of glasses from a tray which materialised at his elbow, and handed her one. "Cheers. Do you drink cocktails?"

"I — not often," she admitted. "Where I come from it's considered a little fast. This one is nice." She was too honest to attempt deception. This man was known to be a hard drinker, hard worker, hard player and the life he lived showed in his face. His name was continually in the news. Six years before he had written a best seller and since that time his pen had seemed dipped in gold.

"And you come from . . . ?" he prompted.

"Westmorland. By the way, I saw your play on television a month ago."

Because she did not praise it he asked: "Well? What did you think of it?"

She hesitated.

"Go on — I don't mind," he was laughing as he tipped the glass to his lips to finish the cocktail.

"I didn't think it was quite up to your usual standard."

"Good for you — I couldn't agree more." He took her empty glass and placed it with his own on a small table. "Evidently a young woman of keen observation. We should get together over this." They discussed the play for several minutes. "I think the psychology was sound enough but the whole action was too hurried; I grant you that. I think I was probably soused when I wrote it." His brief laugh sounded hard. "What do *you* do?"

She wondered if he had resented her opinion. "Nothing much. All the people here seem to do something special . . . even Claribel . . ."

"Claribel . . . what a fascinating name. Tell me, what does Claribel do?"

Louella realised that he was making a mental note of Claribel's catering activities. "She took a Domestic Science degree first, of course. This sort of thing doesn't just happen. You should taste her sausage rolls."

"I'd like to." When he laughed he appeared younger. His sun-tanned face softened and his keen eyes grew gentler. "You still haven't told me what *you* do. I'm interested in people — it's my stock-in-trade."

He must be at least thirty-five, she thought, yet his smile made him seem younger.

"I'm a secretary — or will be when I get my first post. I only arrived in London yesterday and haven't got fixed up yet."

Rosemary came towards them, breaking into the conversation. "Please come, Mr. Charles. I want you to meet everyone."

He turned to her, his eyes flashing in amusement. "I'm coming. I'll see you later, Miss Ford."

Louella nodded and looked about the room for someone she knew. Claribel signalled to her to join her group.

"Louella — Bill, Eric, Connie, Mabs, Brooky — tell us, we're dying of curiosity. What's he like? Does he bite?"

"Eugene Charles? No, he's very nice. Blasé, perhaps — but nice."

Connie opened her wide eyes. "Is that all you can tell us? Why, he's supposed to be charming — and a lady-killer. None of the married boys will let their wives talk to him."

"Don't be hammy," Bill scoffed. "You girls are ridiculous."

"What did you talk about?" Claribel insisted.

"Books — his work — yours, too." Louella's lovely complexion was glowing with colour, her eyes shining, and she was alive again. Gone was the former depression. Eugene Charles had said that he would see her again and she determined to afford him every opportunity.

"Why on earth did you discuss my work?" Claribel was taken aback.

"Because I couldn't think of anything else."

"Safe topic," Mabs suggested and they all laughed jeeringly. "Don't you know he was married. His wife died last year or not long ago. I believe he's free — and looking around."

"He needn't look further than Almira Ashton," Brooky said primly. "She'd have him — if she could get him."

"Meow! Who's talking now? Almira

has had four in a row, and she isn't finding it so easy to get rid of this last one, poor dear. It's all over town, of course, so it's not a secret."

Louella listened attentively, registering every word of the carefree group. This was a different world from the one she had grown up in, and she felt to be out of her depth. Her green eyes followed Eugene everywhere, and he was evidently popular. She drifted towards the door again, when she saw that he was preparing to leave.

"Have you had anything to eat?" Rosemary was everywhere at once. Her soft cheeks were flushed. "Simon is with Eugene, and I believe Eugene has to go soon. He's awfully nice, isn't he?"

They all drifted together. Simon stood with his arm round Rosemary's waist as they chatted. Eugene Charles looked at Louella thoughtfully. There was a calculating look on his face that she resented.

"Know something?" he said. "I'm without a secretary at the moment.

She's on six months' leave; visiting relatives in Australia. The Agency sends me in someone occasionally, but it isn't entirely satisfactory."

She looked up hopefully. "Could I help out — temporarily?"

"It would only be temporary," he warned. "She's a very good secretary and I want her back eventually — mainly because she can spell."

"I can spell too. Try me . . . "

He shook his head smilingly. "You'd better look me up tomorrow — about eleven? Here's my card."

It was so casually done that she was deceived. "You really mean me to call?"

"Yes. Don't you want to?" He waited for her reply, before turning to talk to Simon. Louella stood aside, until he turned to her. "Goodnight." He glanced at her as he made his way to the door, where friends were crowding round to bid him farewell. She looked down at the card in her hand. So he lived on the Embankment. What a wonderful address.

It was after midnight when Louella and Claribel returned to the flat.

"Are you sure you understood him properly?" Claribel yawned. "It sounds almost too good to be true."

"He wouldn't have given me his card if he hadn't wished me to call," Louella pointed out logically, and she knew for certain in her own mind that he had extended the invitation seriously. "This must be my lucky day."

Claribel was sleepy and didn't stay up to argue the matter. She had left the flat the following morning when Louella prepared for her appointment. Dressed in a navy blue woollen dress, with spotless white collar and cuffs and a white straw boater, she studied her reflection in the mirror, longing to look older. But she did look businesslike, she told herself.

If she did not get this post she was going to be disappointed. Was it because she had been interested in his work that Eugene Charles had offered the situation? She thought so.

The big, old-fashioned building before which her taxi stopped, gave no clue to the life within. So many of these old houses held luxury behind the dark walls and windows. She paid the driver and stood for a moment on the pavement before ringing the bell. She drew a long breath. I've got to have this post, she told herself. I've got to make the right impression. She twitched her dress into position, making sure that her appearance was neat. A maid opened the door.

"Oh yes, you are expected." The door opened fully to admit her.

Louella liked the middle aged woman, seeing the old fashioned long hair neatly piled at the back of her smooth head. She wasn't quite the sort of person she had expected to see here. She followed indoors.

"I'll take you into the office. Please come this way."

Louella followed quickly to a room at the end of the big hall. What a huge place it was, with high windows, several doors opening off the hall, and a staircase on the left.

"The young lady to see you, Mr. Charles."

Louella found herself in the study, the door closing after her.

Eugene Charles looked up absently, and she realised that he had been working while he waited. He rose and held out his hand. He looked taller here than he had the previous night. He was in an open necked shirt with a sports coat and grey trousers.

"You are prompt. I like that. Sit down, won't you?"

His long look puzzled her. He had a right to weigh her up if that was the way he felt, but she could not understand the deep concentration of his regard.

He returned to his place behind the mahogany desk and sat down. Louella scarcely dared to allow her attention to wander to the appointments in the beautiful room. Although primarily an office his personality was stamped here. Her gaze came back to his suddenly, when she realised that he had not yet begun the interview.

"You are wanting a secretary . . . " she prompted.

He picked up a pencil, and leaned back carelessly. "Yes. I am. Would you give me your background? Have you references with you? That sort of thing. Where do you come from?"

She opened a neat, white handbag. "I've only one reference, from the firm where I worked as typist before coming to London. I left school at eighteen, went to college for two years, and that's the only place where I've worked." It did not seem enough background to offer in return for this glamorous job, and her heart sank with disappointment.

He scrutinised the letter without comment, before placing it on the blotter in front of him. "There will be other names you could give me. Minister, doctor and so on."

"Oh, yes." She watched him scribble down the names she gave him for reference. "I realise I'm probably not the type of person you are looking for. I've always lived in the country."

"Westmorland you said — what part?"

She named the village. This was necessary, yet she dreaded what he might reveal.

"I know it. I've motored through there a few times. So you come from a quarrying area. We must talk about that sometime. I did a series of articles once for a magazine — but forget that. Would you like to work here? Is this what you had in mind?" His fingers drummed on the desk and she realised again that she was under surveillance.

"Yes — oh, yes."

"My secretary will probably return in about four months. If you care to take on the situation for that length of time, it's yours." His intense concentration made her rebel inwardly. His blue eyes were cold, calculating, utterly baffling, for she could not discover his mood. The closed look held his face, and she realised that he would be a difficult man to know — and to please. "I realise you haven't done any real secretarial work but you can learn, I suppose."

"Thank you. I'd certainly like the chance."

"Then we'll settle for that. Can you be here about nine in the morning? My hours are often erratic but I don't think I'm unduly hard on my staff." He leaned over, picked up a loose folder, opening it wide on the desk. "All this stuff needs typing — think you can sort it out?"

She glanced through the pages, seeing the erasions, her heart sinking. "Yes, I'm quite sure I can."

"All right. That's your desk by the window. Start tomorrow. Now — about salary." He named a sum that she thought was fair and which she accepted.

There was the sound of a scuffle outside the door, and a child's voice was raised indignantly. "No, nanny. You mustn't. Billy isn't ready."

"My daughter," Eugene rose to open the door to admit a child of about three years of age. "You must meet Camille."

"I'm sorry, sir," the nurse apologised.

"I tried to get her past the door without interrupting you, but she evaded me."

"That's all right, nurse. Let her come in for a minute." He lifted the child and brought her to Louella. "This is Camille — darling, my brand new secretary."

Camille was enchanting. She gave Louella a grave, friendly smile.

"How do you do. Daddy — you forgot Billy . . ."

"Of course . . . here, Billy, old man . . ." Eugene urged a dog to come forward. Louella watched the door, but nothing appeared. Camille nodded and spoke soothingly.

"There now, Daddy didn't mean to chop you in two in the door. Did you, Daddy? Poor, poor Billy."

Eugene glanced at Louella, defying her to smile at this imagery. He bent dutifully to pat Billy, at the same time setting the child on her own feet. "Run along with nurse now, dear. Are you going to walk in the park?"

"Yes — and Billy is coming with

us today." Camille shook hands with Louella. "I'm glad you're coming to write Daddy's books for him . . ."

"Thank you." Louella was silenced as they watched the nurse and child leave the house.

"The trouble we have with that blessed dog," Eugene meditated.

"She's a lovely child." They watched through the window until child and nurse disappeared. "Well, I'll come tomorrow — and thank you."

He opened the door for her into the hall. He had the air of someone glad to be done with a situation. "Good-morning."

Louella was out on the pavement again, the door firmly shut upon her. That was all she meant to the great Eugene Charles. She could be useful to him for a time, that was all. Her pulses quickened. What a wonderful house. She longed for the freedom to explore the rooms. It must be so satisfying to live in a house like that again, taking luxury for granted.

"You're evidently one of the lucky

ones," Claribel said at lunch. She was preparing for another afternoon party. "Better to be born lucky than rich, after all going wrong, the luck must be turning. Imagine you meeting his daughter too."

"It's only temporary, but it could lead to something better. Oh, I'm thrilled, Claribel. I really am. Can I help you with anything?"

Claribel soon had her polishing silver, and packing it carefully in the partitioned boxes. "Just be careful, that's all . . . oh, not about the silver . . . about *him* I mean. You haven't heard half the talk there is about him, and how much of it's true, I wouldn't know."

"There is always gossip about anyone as much in the public eye as he is," Louella said. "It's all part of it, if you see what I mean."

"Yes . . . " Claribel sounded doubtful.

Louella arrived on the doorstep the following morning as a clock somewhere in the neighbourhood struck nine. Eugene was not yet up, but she was shown into his study, where the open folder was on her desk. She flicked through the leaves before removing her hat and coat. The pages were badly typed, some hand written, but all were legible. This was her first task and she hoped to acquit herself well. Paper, typewriter, carbon, eraser, all were to hand, and she was well into the first chapter of the novel when Eugene strolled into the room about half-past ten.

He closed the door with a definite bang, and she glanced up.

"Good morning, Miss Ford."

"Good morning, Mr. Charles." He looked as if he had been sleeping off a hangover, she thought. "I've been typing this — it was what you wanted, wasn't it?"

He picked up some of the finished pages. "Good girl. Yes, get on with that, please. I'm going out this morning." He was dressed in a light grey suit and looked elegant and attractive. She watched him as he opened his desk drawer, filled a gold cigarette case, and felt for his note case, checking the contents. "I'm absent minded lately and sometimes land in ridiculous situations, when I haven't a penny in my pocket with which to pay my way. That's one of your jobs — prompting me. By the way, if anyone rings, I'll be in about two o'clock — I think." He glanced in the mirror, caught her gaze and grinned cheerfully. "Sara will put you wise about anything you want to know. Goodbye."

He went out, whistling casually, leaving Louella staring at the door in a trance. She started when the telephone bell shrilled noisily at her elbow. She lifted the receiver and took a deep breath.

"This is Mr. Charles' office."

"Is Eugene there?"

"He has just left for an appointment, and won't be back until about two o'clock. Who is it?"

"It doesn't matter. He's probably on his way here. Did he say where he was going?" The vibrant voice was insistent.

"No. Shall I . . . "

"If we *are* at cross purposes, and

41

goodness knows we seem to have been all this past week, tell him I'm expecting him, will you? This is Almira Ashton speaking." The rich voice gave a distinction and importance to the name that thrilled Louella. She was actually talking to a film actress, and an important one, too.

"Thank you. I'll do that." In a moment the line went dead and she sat back to recover. This might be the first of many contacts with famous people. She might actually meet some of them. Evidently Eugene moved in exalted circles. Was that his real name — or just the name he wrote under?

Lunch was brought to her on a tray by the same middle-aged woman who had greeted her at the door. She stayed to chat for a few minutes.

"Mr. Charles said you were to make yourself at home. After lunch I'm to show you round. In future you could have lunch with Camille and Nurse if you prefer. He's seldom in for lunch of course."

Louella thanked her and enjoyed the

meal provided. Later she was shown round the house. The ground floor held, beside the office, drawing room and domestic quarters, a large library stacked with books. This panelled room was evidently Eugene's special den. Big leather chairs were grouped round the fireplace and the carpet and curtains were in matching green.

"This was the one room he never allowed his wife to change," Sara said primly. "I don't blame him either. She loved the contemporary style and it doesn't always suit these old houses. Come upstairs."

"It's certainly a beautiful room," Louella said.

The front of the first floor was given up to the lounge, where furnishing and decorations were modern. There were three bedrooms on this floor, one of them Eugene's, the others guest rooms. On the floor above Camille reigned supreme, the four rooms given up to her needs. Nurse was preparing her for the afternoon nap so Louella did not linger.

She followed Sara down the stairs again, and presently the woman took away the tray, and Louella settled down again to the afternoon's typing. Seeing his house had made her thoughtful, and she wondered why he had told Sara to show her round. Presently she forgot everything but the pleasure of typing out the unfolding story. She would have recognised Eugene's sure touch here even if she had been unaware that he was the author. He had a vivid, trenchant strength that shone through the written word. He had a gift for bringing a scene to life so that one moved into it, like walking into a painting. One really suffered with his characters.

She started violently when the door opened, for she had been unaware that anyone was near.

Eugene's eyes narrowed as he looked across the room at her flushed cheeks. "You still here? Do you know the time?"

"No." She hoped she did not look as dazed as she felt.

"It's nearly six o'clock. Surely you haven't been at this all day?" His fingers riffled through the neatly stacked pages on her desk.

"I have — and it's been one of the happiest days of my life." She looked up earnestly. "It's your best book so far. How does it end — I can hardly wait to know."

"Really?" His glance was pleased, almost uncertain. For the first time his eyes had lost the calculating look that she disliked so much. "I've been wondering whether to scrap it and start again."

"Oh, no," she spoke impulsively. "This is life. It's held my attention all day, and I forgot I was typing, at a certain disadvantage." Her words were sincere and he accepted them readily.

"Know something? I'm not sure myself how it will end. I never do. If I don't know then it should be a surprise for the reader. But look, there is no need for you to stick to it like this. There is no hurry. Get along home now — and I . . . by the way, did anyone call?"

45

She had been so far away in thought during the afternoon that she had to make a conscious effort to remember. "Why, yes, Miss Ashton phoned, but as she said you would probably be on your way there I didn't think it was important. No one else."

Louella longed to know if he *had* been with Almira Ashton until now, but he did not enlighten her. His smile was charming however when he said "I wonder if I might trespass further on your time after all. I need, someone with whom to discuss that ending. Would you dine with me tonight? Eight? I'll pick you up on my way to the Savoy."

Louella flushed, all the old shyness returning, tempting her to refuse, but she kept back the hasty words. She *would* go. This was all part of her job as secretary to a famous novelist. "Thank you. I'll be ready."

Now that he had her promise he appeared indifferent. "Run along." He prepared to go to the library, and she soon let herself out into the mild evening air. Early summer was her favourite time of the year. Never before had she experienced it in London, and she felt a sudden nostalgia for homelier scenes.

"Claribel . . . " she shouted as she entered the flat. "I'm going to dine at the Savoy with Eugene Charles."

"Why?" Claribel asked disagreeably as she emerged from the kitchen where she was wrestling with their evening meal. "Wish I'd known sooner."

"Sorry — it's to discuss the ending of his latest book. He must want the woman's angle or something. Oh, Claribel I'm so happy. Will my blue dress be good enough. I can't wear the flame again."

"Why not? Hasn't he grasped yet that you're a working girl? But your blue is sweet too. You're really on your way, aren't you? Don't forget the gypsy's warning, will you?"

"I'm not quite sure what you mean by that — but I won't," Louella promised excitedly. "I'll have my bath now, and you needn't cook for me, Claribel. He's calling for me."

"Don't some people have all the luck," Claribel returned to the kitchen and threw the carrot she had been scraping back into the water. Carrots were good, specially when they were grated, but even carrots would be glamorised if eaten at the Savoy. She sighed gently as she traced her name on the wet board. If only she'd had green eyes and shining black hair and a mouth that curled into laughter . . .

"I like your friend," Eugene said when they were in his big car, weaving their way through the traffic.

"So do I. She's real," Louella told him.

"Aren't we all — real?" His glance sideways held amusement.

"Maybe we're all trying to be, but that isn't the same as *being*. Claribel is everything I'd like to be, and probably will never attain." Her sigh was genuine and frustrated, and Eugene's smile faded.

"Do you think any of us see ourselves as we really are?"

"Yes — most women do, anyway. I

48

haven't any illusions about myself. I'm just plain ordinary."

"Ornary, is the American version I believe. Cheer up, you've plenty of time to change. We all go through phases. Life's been made for the living, and if we've any sense we try to live it decently."

"Are you living it decently?" she asked demurely.

"I'll take that question seriously. I honestly don't know the answer right now. I've been going through a phase too, but I'm hoping it's nearly over for me. It seems to me that one phase follows another all through the years and one has to accept them. It's our attitude that counts. If we live fearfully, then it is bound to bring evil towards us. Live courageously — then it attracts good fortune. That's what I call moralising, and we're here — thank God." His sudden change of tone made her laugh outright.

Their table was tucked away at the back of the room, and Louella was glad of this, for she felt nervous, unsure of herself. She was able to survey everyone in the room, and gradually calmed down. She wondered if Eugene had chosen this table with a purpose in view. The room was busy, the waiters discreet and preoccupied and very helpful. Louella was thrilling to the luxury and subdued gaiety of the occasion.

"Now, what'll we have?" Eugene concentrated on her suddenly. In evening dress he made a handsome escort, she thought. She felt the veiled surveillance of his look, and wondered if she was on probation in some way. The idea disturbed her, but she tried to ignore it.

"You choose. This is my first time here — and almost my first public meal in London. I'd hate to order all the wrong things."

He nodded, smiling good naturedly, and she realised that honesty had done more for her than a bold front. "Right. Something light?" He obviously knew how to order a meal for a woman.

Louella was hungry and ate everything

that was placed before her with hearty appetite. It was some time before she realised that their conversation was becoming a routine question and answer, with herself supplying all the answers. Eugene was evidently interested in her background and extracted information disarmingly. He asked about her parents, her family generally. Louella was careful when she realised where his questions were leading her.

"You don't seem too fond of your stepmother," he suggested lightly, taking a mouthful of chicken. "Is she the stock character?"

"I suppose so. Perhaps some of it was my own fault. My own mother was a darling." She put down her fork hastily, looking up into his face. "I'm sure you can't be interested in this kind of thing."

"But I am — I like to know as much as possible about those around me . . . then I can forget it."

Louella's eyes held a warning sparkle. "Why?"

"One day you'll know." He hesitated as if undecided whether to say anything further, but evidently decided against it. "Don't look so belligerent; I'm not prying — I hope."

"I hope so too."

She felt vaguely dissatisfied and pondered the reason. To get them safely away from personalities she said: "You mentioned the island of Gotland earlier. You were there when you wrote your book. Is it a fascinating place?"

"Remarkably so." He warmed to the change of subject instantly. "I stayed in Visby which is a wonderful town. One catches the atmosphere there and it is like no other place I have ever visited. Lots of wonderful ruins, thousands of roses, a well preserved wall round the town . . . everything."

"What was your story about?"

"I'd two sets of characters — ran the reincarnation theme through both sets — worked it down through the ages and found happiness for the lovers of the modern age."

"It must be fun," she said wistfully.

"Actually it was the most difficult book I've ever written. There was a lot of research to be done, and it was not until I visited Visby that the book began to live for me. I think the final scene where the hotel gets on fire, and hero rescues heroine is fairly well done. You see, by this time the reader is supposed to have grasped that the modern lovers *are* the reincarnation of the earlier set who lost each other. Oh yes, you've guessed it — through a fire."

"I hope they do find happiness in the end together?"

"Naturally. It wouldn't be a Eugene Charles' book if they didn't, would it?" he said easily.

"I look forward to reading the book. I believe you said you'd had the proofs?"

"Yes, a few weeks ago."

"It sounds as if it will make a wonderful film . . . "

There was a small commotion of sound and movement, as if someone of importance were arriving, and they both glanced towards the entrance. Coming into the room was one of the loveliest women Louella had ever seen. Her beauty was vivid and sensational. Her colouring was exquisite. She walked with a gliding movement that was a poem in motion. Her gown was guaranteed to arrest the eye if her personality did not. Louella could not takes her eyes off the beautiful woman until she was settled at a table some distance away.

Eugene muttered something under his breath, and she glanced briefly in his direction. "Who is she?"

"You were talking to her on the telephone this morning."

"Almira Ashton?" Louella whispered.

"Yes." They were watching intently as the actress and her two escorts settled down at their table. "That's her stage name of course. Her real name is much more ordinary."

Louella longed to ask what it was, but the guarded look on his face repelled her. He seemed undecided for a moment, but finally rose.

"Will you excuse me? I must speak to her — won't be a moment."

Louella nodded mechanically. Almira Ashton noticed him immediately and signalled imperiously for him to join her table. Eugene lounged across the room unconcernedly, taking his time, his brown face smiling. Louella watched him, wondering that he could appear so casual, almost as if he were deliberately so. Louella gazed down at her plate for a while, until curiosity got the better of her. She was glad to see that the conversation was ending between the two, and he was preparing to return to her. Almira Ashton looked after him pensively, her blue eyes dark and thoughtful. How wonderful to be as beautiful as that.

"I just had to explain why I didn't see her today," Eugene said when he seated himself again.

"She doesn't looked very pleased about something."

He laughed carelessly. "She wasn't. She likes to have her own way in all

55

things — and sulks when she doesn't."

"You must be the only man in London who doesn't let her have it?" Louella suggested. "She's quite fascinating."

"Very. I don't know of a more fascinating woman anywhere. Now, let's talk of something else." He deliberately changed the subject, and she was content to follow his lead. When the meal ended there was little about her that he did not know — but that little she held inviolate. "Your brother is two years younger than yourself — that makes you twenty-two? That's a great age to be. I'm thirty-three."

She wanted to say that he looked older, but dare not. She was puzzled by the situation, not quite at ease within it, and she decided to keep her own council. Her hands gripped together nervously in her lap, and she prayed that he would not follow up her words about Wain. It was so difficult to explain to a stranger. Claribel understood because she knew Wain. Anyone who knew Wain would know that he could not be guilty of robbery with assault.

It was after ten o'clock when they rose to leave the hotel. Eugene gravely helped her on with her satin cape, before they walked to the entrance. "Will you wait here until I get the car — or will you come with me?"

"I'll come." The night was warm, and she was glad to leave the heated atmosphere for the fresher air outside. She felt thoughtful as she accompanied him to the parked car. Very soon they were on their way back to Claribel's flat. It was all so prosaic that she felt a little disappointed. She wondered if she ought to ask him in, but decided against this, as he was her employer after all. Just what he thought he had gained from her society she did not know, although they had discussed at least one of his novels. His casualness baffled her.

"Thank you for an excellent meal and a — pleasant evening."

He laughed, turning on the charm for her special benefit. He knew what she meant. "Goodnight. I'll see you tomorrow."

"Yes. Goodnight."

Claribel was waiting up for her, agog to hear what had occurred. "It sounds to have been what he said earlier — he just wanted to get to know you better. Well, how do you like the new boss at close quarters?"

"Very much. He's really a nice person." Louella told her about Almira Ashton's entrance. "She walks like this — as a Queen is supposed to walk, only more so. Now why can't I focus every eye on me and make a grand entrance?"

"That kind of thing takes years of practice, my sweet," Claribel smiled disagreeably, and yawned until her jaws cracked. "I'll bet our Almira isn't a day under thirty-five either — and all that much poise comes with age — or didn't you know?"

"Is she really as old as that? She doesn't look it. Eugene is thirty-three; he told me so."

"Now wasn't that nice?" Claribel

murmured sarcastically. "He looks older."

"Well, he isn't. Don't you like him, Claribel?"

"Sure I do. Go on — tell Claribel. I can keep secrets — I think."

"I think she's in love with him."

"What's stopping her? He's not married at the moment — or is he?"

"No. His wife died. You sound thoroughly unpleasant, dear Claribel, and it's way past your bedtime. None of it is my business really."

"But isn't it interesting?" Claribel yawned again. "I wonder if she'll get him. She's been married four times."

"That's not many really — or is it? Film stars seem to be apart from real life. If she loves Eugene then they'd probably marry." The thought was confusing and did not fit in anywhere. "Goodnight, Claribel. Don't yawn so much or your jaws may lock."

Claribel gave her an offended look before taking herself off to bed.

When Louella arrived at the house the

following morning, Eugene was already hard at work. His presence unsettled her for a while, until she realised that he wished to be quiet. He was concentrating on the last chapter, and evidently well into his stride, for they did not speak once after the first greeting. He smoked incessantly, completely engrossed, and after a while she was able to forget him, and proceed with her own routine work. He had told her that when the present novel was complete, he would probably dictate future work. That meant she must brush up her shorthand. Her fingers tapped the keys happily through the hours as once more the narrative captured her imagination.

Somewhere a clock struck twelve, and she glanced up, surprised. Eugene was leaning back in his chair, watching her quietly. Evidently he had just put down his fountain pen. His gaze flicked away and he rose to saunter towards her desk.

"I believe you really are interested in this?" he said gravely, picking up the top sheet. "I've just finished the first draft — unless I get a better idea."

"Really? It is wonderful to have this gift, Mr. Charles . . . "

"Don't you think we might drop the formality — when we are alone, at any rate. My friends mostly call me Gene."

"Do they?" She felt too shy to comply at once. "All right."

"Go on, Louella, tell me what you think of the novel — complimentary or otherwise. I can take it." His pleasant manner held something studied that she could not define. She was confused and too inarticulate to continue. "All right. I won't press the point. I'm going out now. If anyone calls tell them I'll not be back until about five — or later. I'll be walking . . . "

Probably the ending of his novel would be thought out during the walk. Louella could understand that any author would need to be alone. She had not helped him much, she remembered, as she stared at the closed door.

Day followed day as Louella typed her way to the end of the novel. She was completely engrossed, and would have missed lunch had not Sara brought it to her each day. During the morning hours she would meet Eugene, but seldom after lunch, for he had a complete life away from the house. She felt happier than she had for months, and more secure in the knowledge that she was standing on her own feet. There was a charm within this big house, a quietness that even Camille did not break with her child's laughter.

"I think it's a happy house," Louella told Claribel on one occasion.

"Eugene must be a good tempered man — is that why?"

"I — don't know. Probably he is." Even to herself she could not sum up the atmosphere. She settled down so completely that it was quite a surprise to her when Eugene called her into his study one day, about eleven o'clock.

He rose as she entered, and closed the door after her. "I thought we could talk better in here." He placed a chair for her, facing the window and opposite to his own position. "Can I have your full attention, please."

Her heart sank beneath the gravity of his tone, and she wondered in which duty she had been remiss.

"I've had answers to the letters I wrote to your sponsors . . . and they are satisfactory."

She was jarred into awareness, and looked at him expectantly. Today she was wearing a yellow and white silk dress, which suited her dark colouring. He had gone to so much trouble to check on her, when he only offered a temporary post. The thought disturbed her again. "I didn't know you had written . . . " she said in a worried voice.

"I did — at once. How long have you been with me now? Almost three weeks." He was smiling reassuringly. "Cheer up, Louella."

They both smiled, and she waited for his next words.

"I suppose I've taken more care over this matter than seems necessary on the face of it to you, but I had my reasons. I don't quite know how to put what I have to say — but will you hear me through before you judge?"

"Yes." Evidently the bank manager, the minister, had not mentioned Wain and his disgrace. Of course they wouldn't — and it was obvious that Eugene did not guess what had happened.

He drew a photograph in a silver frame out of a drawer and passed it to her. "That is a photograph of my wife — she died over two years ago."

Louella took the photograph with both hands, scanning it curiously. Eugene watched her silently.

"Well?"

She looked across at him. "She — she's not unlike me, is she?"

"She is extraordinarily like you, Louella. The only difference is that you have green eyes, and hers were blue. I tell you, the likeness shook me when we first met."

She looked at the photograph again, knowing the reason for that earlier surveillance.

"She was my secretary before we married; we were happy too. I'd like to assure you on that point. We cared for each other. Her death devastated me, but I've tried to pull myself together. It's taken two years . . . Are you engaged, Louella?"

"I was . . . "

"Not any more? I thought I hadn't noticed you wearing a ring . . . "

"I was engaged to Clunes Syke for several months . . . "

"What happened? Don't you care for him now?" His alertness helped her.

"I don't know — but I wouldn't marry him if he were the last man on earth. I just — couldn't . . . "

"May I ask why?"

"You may — but I wouldn't answer."

He laughed in genuine amusement. "Fair enough. It's none of my business . . . although it has a bearing on what I want to say."

They measured glances, Louella on the defensive because she felt complete loss of confidence. Why was he telling

65

her these things? She knew that he *had* felt his wife's death keenly; Sara had told her so. It was a well-known fact too, that it took a couple of years to recover from a deep loss. She drew a deep breath to steady herself.

"You'll marry — in time . . . " His casual words vexed her.

Impetuously she burst into explanation. "Life is too interesting. I want to make something of myself. I mean to become rich and successful. There just isn't room in my life now — for love . . . "

The words evidently checked him, for he appeared to hesitate. Louella felt his uncertainty, and pondered the cause. His fingers drummed on the book as if his thoughts were far away. "That sounds to be quite a statement for a girl like you. It's not like you — you're so gentle."

"You don't know me very well," she suggested, wondering if this would be the end of the post she had valued so much. This was to have been the first rung of the ladder for her, and already she was failing. Her heart sank with sudden depression. She wanted to be sophisticated and hard but it was difficult when her heart insisted in being heard.

"You forget that I'm a shrewd judge of character. It's all part of my job. I make quick decisions about people and am not often proved wrong. I don't think I'm wrong now, in spite of your words."

She felt deeply troubled, as uncertain in her turn as he had been. There had been friendship between them from the first, yet her own handling of the situation had held him away, she knew.

The silence lengthened until she began to feel uncomfortable. Glancing up into his brown face she surprised a strange look there.

"Are we misunderstanding each other, Louella?" His voice was gentle as if he sought to placate her in some way. "Perhaps I should take this more slowly but . . . I'm hoping you'll understand. I want to marry again — to marry you, if you'll have me." The colour beneath his tan deepened and she knew that he was not as calm as he appeared on the surface.

Confusion made her sound brusque. "Why?"

"Really, Louella — the usual reasons. I like you. It's more than that."

"But we don't love each other." She realised the implication behind her words. Although professing not to believe in love, she spoke as if it must be the basis of marriage.

His glance met her anxious one, and he seemed to relax. "I believe we could be happy together. I've — liked you from the first meeting."

She knew that there had been something between them, but honesty forced her to admit the truth. "I'm afraid I don't feel the same way." His life was uncomplicated; he would never understand all the factors behind her reluctance. She thought about Clunes silently, feeling cold and frightened. How could one stop loving a person, even when one's mind denied one's heart the right to that love?

He sighed. "I wish I could change

your attitude. Perhaps I've spoken too soon after all?"

"I don't know. I thought . . . " she hesitated, her gaze on the wall behind his head. "Everyone says . . . "

He was amused by her hesitation. "So many people say so many things that I no longer listen to public opinion. Say what is in your mind."

"Surely Miss Ashton will soon be divorcing her husband . . . " She realised her mistake instantly, and regretted it.

"What has that to do with me? With this discussion?"

She was unable to answer, floundering in a pool of thought that held a secret beneath the surface.

"I don't know all that's in your mind, but will you try to believe I'm sincere now? I've felt drawn to you from our first meeting in Rosemary's house. At first it was just — interest, then I knew it was more than that. I wanted you — as my wife. Others do not enter this at all."

"I thought Miss Ashton did," she said presently.

He stiffened with displeasure. Louella felt appalled by her own words but they could not be recalled. Surely he must know that there could be no answering emotion from her? Too much was unexplained between them.

"I think you should wait . . . " she said.

"It's not so easy — when you're completely bewitched by a woman — in fact it's deuced hard."

She shook her head, trying to clear her mind of the things he was saying. "I don't understand you at all. Why don't you marry her and get it out of your system? It seems quite uncomplicated to me. Marry someone and become disillusioned — that's the way."

"You're not thinking straight. Listen to me, Louella. I don't want to make a mistake. Camille is very dear to me. My way of life is pleasant. I don't see where Almira would fit in, do you? Apart from every other consideration I refuse to be Mr. Five — possibly one of a succession of husbands. Almira is an enchantress, spoiled, delightful, selfish, utterly without moral scruple — and she wouldn't fit in here, would she?"

"Is it that you don't wish to be a doormat for her?" she asked shrewdly.

He shrugged, not too pleased with the question. "If I'm married that puts marriage with her completely out of the picture, doesn't it?"

So that was his reasoning? She gazed at him thoughtfully. "You can't turn off an emotion as strong as love just by marrying someone else," Louella whispered. His words had shocked her, knocking at some core of integrity within her character for which she could not account.

"I have no intention of marrying Miss Ashton," he said firmly. "You will treat this matter in complete confidence I hope?"

"Oh, yes." She felt dazed, and unsure of her own feelings. "Then listen to me again, Louella. I think we could be happy together. Don't you care for the idea?"

Did he realise how great was the

temptation, she wondered miserably.

"I would be generous — make you a marriage settlement of two thousand pounds, if that is enough? You would be hostess at all the parties and receptions I must give. There are difficulties for a man trying to manage alone. You would travel with me, in all ways be my wife."

"I don't love you . . . " she whispered despairingly.

"I realise that. Shall we compromise? Let us marry almost at once, but for six months we'll just be friends, getting to know each other. I'm willing to wait if it means a better understanding eventually. Is that fair?"

She thought of all the parts of the situation, the difficulties that would be solved if she agreed. "Make it twelve . . . " she said recklessly.

"Six. That's too long in my opinion, but I realise I've been hasty."

Could she bring herself to accept such a proposal? Six months was a long time, and anything might happen. "Suppose at the end of that time we can't stand the sight of one another?"

He laughed grimly, half turning away. "We can settle that if — and when it comes up."

She felt his disappointment like a tangible thing between them and wondered the cause. "Aren't you afraid you may meet someone else?"

"Aren't you?" His coldness baffled her, and she realised that his anger was stirring beneath her lack of confidence. "Don't get the wrong idea into your head, Louella. I'm warning you here and now — I don't believe in divorce, so that's out for us if we take this step. I shall do my utmost to make you care for me. I intend to succeed."

She kept her gaze lowered, feeling distressed. "Is that why you will not consider marrying Miss Ashton?" What a strange man he was, so much deeper than he appeared on the surface. He had made his decision.

"Could be. Listen Louella, this is between us — not anyone else. Will you give me your answer, please?"

She continued to stare down at the floor, overcome by an emotion she could not name.

Wain's face drifted before her. Thin, young, anxious, a shadow over him, that only she could lift. She knew her decision was taken.

"I agree."

He turned back to her from the window, his manner pleased and brisk. "Good. I'll make all the arrangements. I'd like it to be kept as quiet as possible until the wedding day. You'll not change your mind?"

"I promise." She stood up, looking at him blankly.

"I promise, too," he told her. "I always keep my promises. I'll respect our agreement — for six months."

She drew a long, free breath. "Thank you." She tried to listen to the rest of his plans but it was difficult. She returned to the flat earlier than usual, her mind in chaos. What would Claribel say now? She knew that her friend would not approve,

74

and she would not blame her. Yet what she contemplated would help to solve so many difficulties. Wain would be her first care, and she could do so much for him . . .

Her heart grew lighter as she realised all that she could do when the money was hers.

Claribel was entertaining a guest. They both looked up when Louella withdrew her key from the outer door and entered.

The man was tall, and broad, attractive in appearance. Louella thought she would faint with the shock of recognition.

"Clunes . . . you here . . . "

How had he found her? Her father had promised secrecy regarding her address.

"Are you glad to see me, Louella darling?" The musical voice had never sounded more caressing.

2

"I'LL leave you two alone," Claribel offered uncertainly. "You'll want to talk. I quite like your Clunes . . ." she added, passing Louella with a warm smile.

Clunes was standing awkwardly, his gaze fixed on Louella, while he turned his tweed hat in his hands several times. At home he always wore a deerstalker, she recalled. His hair was almost as dark as her own, and he carried a good colour, looking fresh and healthy.

She tried not to show her dismay and surprise. "I don't think that we shall have much to say to each other," she spoke coldly.

"Just the same . . ."

"Don't worry — I'm going." Claribel vanished with speed, ending an embarrassing situation. Clunes had been there half an hour, waiting for Louella to arrive and in that time he had gained Claribel's sympathy. She liked him for his quiet determination.

"Well?" Louella looked at him levelly.

"Let's not quarrel. I'm here to ask if we can't be friends again."

"Impossible. You knew it was the end . . . "

"We all say things when we are angry, and later wish we hadn't." His deep chested figure was closer now as he moved between her and the door. She felt his personality, strong and quiet.

"I'm sorry, Clunes, but I don't feel any different, and I don't wish anything unsaid. I only wish I'd said more so that you would not be here today. I meant every word."

He lighted a cigarette. "Don't you think you are in danger of dramatising the situation a little?"

"No, I don't think so."

"You don't grant me any right to my own opinion?"

"But I do — you have every right to the stand you took; I've no quarrel with you on that score. It's just that I could never agree with your opinion. I happen to know and believe that Wain is innocent. You don't. You said so. That's the difference. It's simple really — and utterly separating. We'd never be happy with so much between us." Her words came coldly.

"Yet you still love me," he suggested, watching her.

"I did — I don't think I do any longer."

"Liar. Louella, let's not stir up any more mud. I don't want to quarrel with you again. We were happy together before all this happened. I want us to get back to that. I care for you; just how much I realised when you vanished. You're the girl I want, and no difference of opinion is going to change that." He was close to her, and she wondered if he meant to touch her, but she gave him no lead.

In the brief silence she moved away. "Is that all you came to say?"

"Well — partly."

"What else?"

He sighed with vexation. "You knew I was to have an audition on the air? It's this week — tomorrow, in fact. I hoped you'd be interested."

She did remember. He had a rich baritone voice and his ambition was to sing his way to prosperity. "I hope you'll be successful. You're on your way, aren't you, Clunes?"

"I hope so, but it won't be very happy if I have to travel alone. Won't you forgive and forget, darling? I want you so much. The future looks grim without you. You know we got on well — before this trouble. We could again. Let's not make a mistake that will involve both our futures, just because . . . "

"Because a principle is involved?" He was not the man to plead and she realised what this interview was costing him. To end it she said, and her words rang with feeling: "Answer me one question honestly. Have you changed your opinion in any way since that evening?"

He hesitated, glanced away from her earnest face.

"You see? You haven't, you know you haven't. Nothing has changed. You still believe deep in your heart that Wain is guilty. I don't believe he is; I never could."

He moved sharply, seeing the tears gather in her eyes. "Look, let's not blind ourselves to realities. I admire your faith in Wain — I reckon I'd feel the same if he were my brother. But facts are facts. Can't you see what you are doing when you carry your faith to these lengths? I'm offering you marriage, your whole future is involved — and mine. We're in love with each other . . ."

"Not any more," she reminded him bleakly. "Something died when you said . . . when you told me . . . "

"Then you have never loved me."

"I did, but we couldn't be happy now, Clunes. This would come up every time we quarrelled — it might be the cause of our quarrels. No, let's stand by the break. You'll recover quite soon, one does, you know. Hearts are resilient." The bitterness of her voice displeased him and he turned aside angrily.

"I hate to hear you talk this way. What's come over you? Claribel hinted that you had changed, and you sure have. Will nothing I can say change your mind? Let me hold you . . . "

"Never. Don't you dare touch me." She wanted to tell him about Eugene, and her promise to marry him, but realised that the time was not opportune. In spite of his forbearance, and appearance of calmness Clunes was a hot-tempered man. So far he had been moderate, almost apprehensive, but she knew not to try him too far. His manner was disappointed and she wondered if he had expected her to come running back into his arms. I'm made of sterner stuff than that, she thought. I don't need Clunes in my life. He hasn't changed, either. People don't change fundamentally. "I don't feel that anything is to be gained by just standing here arguing over old ground. I'm sorry, but I'm not prepared to change. How did you get this address?"

He grinned, swinging round to the window again. "From your father — by a trick. He's worried about you, Louella — and I kept him talking. You should write to him. He sends his love and begs you to write. Remember, he's lost both you and Wain. Tough on the old man." His voice was warmly persuasive again.

"He should have thought of that, shouldn't he? I'll certainly write to him — I meant to as soon as I was settled. I'm not enjoying this either, you know."

"Claribel tells me you've already got a job?"

"Yes." Her soft lips closed firmly on the word. He was giving up, bowing to her wishes, not forcing the issue at the moment, and she wondered what could be in his mind. It was so unlike Clunes to give way. "Shall we be able to hear you on the air tomorrow?"

"I think so. I'm singing with an orchestra, half-past seven, if they decide they like my style."

"It's your chance. I hope you have every success." Once they would have been jubilant, now there was nothing.

"Thank you." He picked up his hat and turned to the door. She saw that he was angry, probably very angry, but his control was superb. He had not intended being dismissed. Their gaze met briefly and she was appalled by the red-hot passion in his eyes. She backed away from him in sudden fear. She had never seen him like this before. For the first time she appreciated his side, and felt ashamed.

He hesitated with his hand on the door knob. "Sure you won't change your mind? I'm not the patient type — you knew that."

"Quite sure."

"It feels like a blasted nightmare," he said violently. "I love you. Doesn't that count?"

"Go — please go." She bent her face into both hands, overcome. Was she sending away the realities and striving to cling to the illusions? She was uncertain and afraid. "I can't bear any more."

"All right I'll go — but I'm coming back, when we're both calmer. You're making a terrible mistake, and I understand because I love you. I respect your feeling for Wain, but what he can give you in the future won't make up for all you're losing. Think it over. I'll see you after the broadcast. Goodnight."

He made no attempt to kiss her, for which she was thankful. Contact might have undermined her resolution. She cried quietly until Claribel came in from the kitchen.

"Gone? Somehow I thought . . . " Claribel bit back the words she had thought. "There was I making twice as much salad as we usually eat. Isn't he staying on for a meal?"

"No — but he's coming back, after the broadcast. Oh, what shall I do? What shall I do?" It was comparatively easy to plan one's whole life and future when emotion was absent, but so difficult when one's heart insisted on having its way.

Was Clunes right? He was so sure that

she still loved him. While that was so her judgment was faulty. She had planned without him, yet he was there, the real menace to her future.

Claribel fluttered about the room uneasily, wondering what to say. "If you don't love him enough, then he'll have to accept it . . . "

"That must be it. I love him — but not enough," Louella agreed.

"Poor Clunes," Claribel spoke in a gentle voice, for she liked Clunes. He was of the earth, strong, masculine, dogmatic. So completely different from Eugene Charles' type. Eugene was physically fit, of course, but he had a deeper intelligence and perception . . . now why on earth was she comparing the two men, she thought uneasily. It had nothing to do with her. The change wasn't in Clunes either — but in Louella. Even I can't understand the change in Louella, she thought. I'll talk to Clunes and try to make him see . . . there must be something I can do . . .

Louella dried her eyes. "Eugene

Charles asked me to marry him today."

Claribel almost choked on the mint she had popped in her mouth. "No? You must be joking."

"I'm sure I'd be surprised too in your place. It's true."

"Have you agreed?" Claribel's colour was coming up in surprise.

"Yes."

"Did you tell Clunes?"

"No — I couldn't. It's all been so sudden."

"You're telling me! Really, you take my breath away. What's behind it? I feel bewildered. Are you in love with him?"

"Listen, don't get excited. The wedding is to be in about three weeks' time. I hope you'll do the catering. Think what the publicity will do for you. I shall insist."

Claribel sat down abruptly. "I said — were you in love with Eugene?"

"No. Lots of people marry without being in love, don't they?"

"Not if they're wise," Claribel said crisply. "What's behind it?"

"He says he's liked me from our first meeting. I had to believe his sincerity. It wouldn't be possible without that."

"But it's all over town that he's mad about Almira Ashton." There were two angry flanges of colour in Claribel's cheeks. "I can't work it out."

"He evidently doesn't think that Miss Ashton will fit into his life. Don't look so shocked, Claribel."

"I hope you know what you're doing."

"He — he's agreed to our being friends only for six months."

"And you fell for that?" Claribel said angrily. "I don't know who he's in love with, but if you get in his way then it's God help you. You're not dealing with a boy now, Louella. Can't you see what will happen? He'll either hate the sight of you — or you'll hate him . . . for different reasons. I'd like to know what's behind all this — so I would."

Louella respected her friend's opinion, and felt deeply troubled, yet she could not dismiss the subject as Claribel was doing.

"I — I hope you won't try to interfere . . . "

"It's none of my business, but you'd better let your father know, hadn't you?"

"Yes, I will later on, but no one can change my mind."

"Why on earth you can't be normal and accept Clunes when he's more than ready to crawl at your feet . . . "

"Clunes has hurt me too much, Claribel. I can't tell even you just why I'll never marry him."

"Yet you love him — and he's crazy to marry you."

"How long would that last?" Louella asked cynically.

"There must be more to your agreeing to marry Eugene than you've explained," Claribel suggested patiently. "I'll never believe . . . " She broke off to add: "Does he know about Wain's trouble?"

"No. Do you think I should tell him?"

Claribel's lips hardened in a tight line. "Don't come to me for advice for you won't take it."

"Listen — try to see it my way. I honestly believe that Eugene is sound, and he has convinced me of his feeling for me. I wouldn't go into this otherwise — but there is something more, and it finally decided me. He is making a marriage settlement of two thousand pounds. Don't you see how that changes everything? I wouldn't do it for myself, but I can for Wain. I need money so desperately so that I can help him. One day I know he's going to need my help and I must be ready. Clunes has no patience with him, or inclination to help him, and there is no one else. I'm the only one who can ever help Wain now. Oh, Claribel, try to understand. This is my chance to change our lives. I don't think I'm wrong. What I'm doing is from a good motive anyway." Tears rose in her eyes as she made her earnest plea for understanding. "I must help Wain."

Claribel considered her words silently. Certainly there was sound feeling behind her recklessness. She knew the feeling that had bound the family together for twenty years. It could not be broken in a few months. Louella's first thought was for her brother.

"What will you do if the marriage fails?" she spoke more gently.

"It may not. I like him so much, Claribel." It was said timidly and suddenly Claribel's stormy face cleared.

"You've given me indigestion — must be the shock." Perhaps the situation would resolve itself without help from anyone. She meant to press Clunes to come often so that Louella would have a chance to change her mind before it was too late.

"I shan't interfere," she promised stiffly. "But I think you're messing up your life — and for what? You don't care for Eugene."

Louella's face was sad and strained as she pondered silently. She would advertise for Wain, she told herself. "Otherwise he may never be traced," she said aloud. "If only I knew where he was."

"If he turns up — before the wedding

— will you go on with it?" Claribel asked after a while.

"Yes, when it comes. I feel suspended somehow — waiting for something terrible to happen . . . "

"I guess you're contributing your share to what's likely to happen," Claribel spoke crossly. "I have a feeling Wain isn't in this country."

"He hasn't enough money to leave it — that's why I'm so certain he is still in England." Louella's clear gaze met Claribel's, holding her off, defying her to say more.

Louella would never be convinced, and Claribel could not blame her for being loyal. Somewhere within the situation was a gleam, a small shoot that might yet save them all from tragedy. Yet the facts must be faced immediately, and Claribel knew that Wain *might* have left the country with the stolen money.

It was all very distressing, and it was best to say as little as possible. Claribel's nature was too large and generous, not to try to help Louella in whatever decision she made.

"I'll be around," she promised. "Do whatever you think is best."

"Thank you."

Louella was to continue in her secretarial capacity until a few days before her wedding to Eugene Charles. Then she would move into the big house on the Embankment for a time.

"We're going abroad later," Eugene said the following morning.

Louella felt quiet and dull, after a sleepless night. She was not able to respond to the ready-made plans.

"You've not changed your mind, have you?" Eugene said quietly. "I've already fixed everything."

She decided to be as frank with him as possible, and told him how Clunes had reappeared, and the outcome of their interview of the previous evening. "I never really expected to see him again. No, I shan't change my mind."

She needed the money he offered as a marriage settlement, and wondered if he knew this was the reason for her compliant attitude.

If he did, would he feel anything but contempt for her in time? She was too mentally tired to follow the thought, as she listened to him outlining his immediate plans.

Later she had her lunch with Camille and the nurse, making friends with the little girl, who was generous and affectionate.

"Daddy says you will be coming with us when we go on holiday," Camille said. "We have fun and swim and do things, don't we, Nanny?"

"Yes, dear." Nanny gave Louella a probing look of enquiry. "*Are* you going on holiday with us?"

"I may be. Nothing is settled yet."

Later, in the office, she continued typing the manuscript, completing the work, leaving it on the desk for Eugene to go through later. She picked up a photograph that was on the shelf above his chair, and gazed at it earnestly for some minutes. It showed Eugene with his wife, and they looked happy and carefree. Louella thought his face was strong, dependable, but you couldn't really judge just from a photograph. His wife had been small, dainty, as dark as Louella herself. What had *she* thought of the association between Eugene and Miss Ashton?

Perhaps she had not known of it — or was it of more recent growth since her death? Surely Eugene would not have cared for Almira Ashton while his wife lived?

She put the photograph into position, uneasily aware that she knew remarkably little about the man whose wife she was to become. Blind trust could not be enough.

Was he with Miss Ashton now? Where did he go when he was absent from the house? His was a mysterious personality. His preoccupation must often stem from his work, for no one could write continuously as he did, without hours of concentration and thought. Louella wondered how she would cope when they were married. Of course it would really be no business of hers. Eugene had made the situation acceptable to her, and he was paying well for the privilege of having his child cared for. Louella knew it was more than that, for his words had held the ring of truth.

"Oh, I wish I could be sure — that he meant all he said . . . "

She was musing in the waning sunshine, her work finished for the day, when Eugene arrived briskly. He threw his hat onto her desk.

"Hullo. Finished? I'll run through that tonight. You might parcel it in the morning and take it round to the publishers. If they get their hands on me I'll be loaded with another batch of work and I need a break. Can't be bothered for a couple of weeks. I've something else on my mind, too. Are you tired? Knock off whenever you like."

She smiled beneath his enthusiasm, for he was in a good mood. "I'm going home now — unless you want to work."

"No, I'm going out for the evening.

Escorting the beautiful Miss Ashton to the première of her new film." He said this deliberately, as if determined to see her reaction.

Louella smiled. "A glamorous occasion?"

"Yes. Almira seems to think that my presence is vital — author and star — good publicity anyway." He said this with a calculating look that made Louella feel like hitting him. Did he use everyone he met to further his own purpose? But wasn't she doing that too, she asked herself wildly. She was going into this with her eyes wide open, her mind made up implacably.

"I'll go," she murmured. "Camille asked me to remind you that you promised to tuck her up tonight before going out."

He followed her to the door, and held it for her to pass through. "Thanks — I'd forgotten. Louella . . . there's nothing wrong, is there? You're not worried about — anything?"

"Of course not. Goodnight." She was eager to escape into the cool evening light. Her mind raced ahead of her in eagerness to hear Clunes singing over the air. He was to be the guest star, and a certain amount of build-up had prepared the way. Louella hoped that he would be a success. He had sung so often before the public that it should not take any special effort to sing before the unseen audience.

She thought of his dark, handsome face, his colourful personality, his colossal strength, and felt herself go weak by comparison. They had known each other for years, yet it was only a year since he had fallen deeply in love with her. The violence of his need had surprised her, and she wondered why it was they had not been married long ago. It would have solved so much if only they had, she thought. All the conflict would have been groundless, because she would have been his wife.

Claribel was out, when Louella entered the flat, and she sat alone, listening intently to every item until Clunes was announced, when she turned up the set. He sang with superb artistry, with confidence, his voice as clear as if he were in the room with her. How often had they sat together, planning for the time when his chance should come? Now it was here and Louella knew that he was heading for success, with or without her. The ballad he sang, was popular, completely right for his début.

When Claribel entered, Louella was crying, her dark head down on the satin cushions. She surveyed the scene for a moment in surprise.

"Clunes? You still love him, don't you? Why not admit it?"

"What's the use?" Louella blew her nose and straightened her hair. The outlook was dreary, but she determined not to give in. "You must be tired, I'll get a meal going."

"Expecting anyone tonight?" Claribel demanded.

"No — not particularly." Louella went into the kitchen to wash her hands and face before starting the meal.

Claribel followed her. "Do you know what I heard today — I believe it's in the evening papers, too." She glanced at Louella quickly. "Your Eugene and Almira Ashton, I mean. She's to star in another of his books — the one about Visby on the island of Gotland. They are going on location soon — together, I imagine. Did he say anything about it?"

"No — why should he?" Louella asked. Was that the reason for his brisk, pleased manner tonight? "That's in the Baltic, isn't it?"

"He's in the money, anyway," Claribel spoke dryly. "Here's the paper — you'll find it in the gossip column."

"Thank you. I'll read it after the meal." Louella placed the paper on the formica topped table, and reached for the vegetables.

Later she read the colourful account in the paper. On the face of it Eugene's life seemed very successful and pleasant. When was he going?

She asked him that question almost as soon as they met the following morning in his office.

"Ah, you read that para?" he was

smiling. "Read well, I thought."

"Is it true?" Louella watched him calmly.

"Yes — partly. Miss Ashton is to star in my book, and I'll probably be on the island part of the time. In fact, I hoped we could go together you and I. Depends . . . on several things."

"I don't understand you." If he was Almira's lover, surely he would not wish to be cluttered with Louella's presence? The situation was baffling, and she longed to shake him in order that he might reveal what was in his mind.

"Wouldn't you like to go?" he suggested.

"In many ways — yes — but not to be played off against — her . . ." Louella choked on the words.

"Who suggested that you would?" His eyes were like ice.

She turned aside, trembling with an emotion she had not experienced before. "Will you — were you meaning to take Camille along, too — and nurse? Was it there you planned to have the holiday?"

"No. One doesn't mix business with

pleasure to that extent. If you don't wish to come with me — say so. I don't know what we're both getting steamed up about — do you?" The careless words belied the look on his face. Suddenly he thrust a hand through his hair, making the ends stands up. "Oh, Lord . . . what's it all about? I thought we understood each other better than this."

"I don't understand anything, any more," she said in a tone that made him smile.

"All I wish to know is if you would care to visit Gotland with me? I was there months ago when I first drafted the book — feeling browned off, too. I'd like to go again under happier circumstances. What's so odd about that?"

"Nothing," she murmured unhappily.

"Right." His face was still closed, and she knew that he was not wholly frank with her, although on the surface he appeared so. "Tracey and I were pretty happy — it's that sort of arrangement I'm after now. I told you I want a wife, not a secretary." His glance played over her. "You appeared to understand."

She turned away, distressed, her whole body trembling. "We were to get to know each other — six months you said — "

"Yes. What's wrong with that?"

She clenched her hands, suddenly determined to tell him. "How can I take the place of your wife when I know the position? This isn't fun. Miss Ashton will know . . . "

He swung her round so that she faced him, and he was tight lipped with anger. "What's the matter with you? Why should Miss Ashton know about our private affairs? Why should she?"

"You should know . . . "

"Then you're believing all the rubbish you read in the papers. Who has been filling your head with that tosh? I'd like to know."

"You must admit your names are linked . . . "

"And how many others? Dozens I should imagine. Almira Ashton's life must be full of men — I'm one of many. Can't you see? I don't want to be singled out. I won't be manœuvred into a position where . . . " he stopped abruptly, and dropped his hands from her shoulders. "Well, it's up to you. Do we go or — don't we?"

"It's not my choice . . . how could it be? I'll do what you wish, within the bounds of reason."

He swore in sudden anger. "Knowing you I don't like the sound of that. All right — we'll not go."

"Can't you go alone as you'd planned?"

"I'll think about it. Evidently we're not advancing along similar lines. I'd hoped for co-operation and hadn't realised you were so obtuse; or is this something else?"

She kept her face turned away so that he would not see her expression. "Don't you want Miss Ashton to hear about your marriage?"

The look he gave her baffled her anew. "No. Not until it's accomplished. I don't care what publicity there is — once we're married. Does that answer your question?"

Her dark head came up proudly. "It does — in more ways than one."

"All right. Let's get down to business. You'll live here afterwards. Do you need cash for immediate necessities?"

She shook her head, finding his handling of the situation hard to bear. She knew that her resistance had angered him.

"The ceremony will be as quiet as possible. Would you like to invite your family? One or two friends, perhaps?"

"I don't think so. I told you I'd left home — and I don't know where my brother is just now." She drew a breath of relief when he did not press the point. "Just Claribel, I think. Afterwards couldn't she do the catering? You want a big party in the evening and she is used to that sort of thing."

"All right. We'll have lunch at an hotel earlier. I want you to buy a magnificent dress to wear that night. I want you to outshine every woman in the room. Think you can manage it?"

"More publicity?" she said recklessly. "I can try."

"I don't want you to say later that I've misled you."

"I won't do that." Her voice was low.

"Let's try to be friends, Louella. I'm not a bear. If you treat me fairly we'll get on very well. I wouldn't go into this if I didn't think so." He held out his hand in a charming gesture, all the chill leaving his thin face.

Louella placed hers in it, trying to meet his keen glance. She felt the tingle of feeling that ran up her arm as his fingers closed over hers in a strong grip.

"That's better. I'm not always in a bad temper, you know. How about yours? Do you fly off the handle easily?" He was laughing as he spoke, drawing her closer with a slow movement.

"Not very easily. I can stand anything so long as I know where I'm going," she agreed, and she answered his smile.

"We can make this anything we wish," he said earnestly. "It's up to us. Just be honest with me in all ways, and you won't find me hard to put up with. Feeling better?"

She wondered how he had known of her mental conflict, that she had been almost sick with worry and strain. "Yes, thank you. And if you want me to go to Visby with you, of course I'll go. I — trust you . . . "

His expression was kindly, almost gentle. "Thank you, Louella. We're beginning to understand each other, aren't we?"

In time, would they attain to a genuine friendship and respect? She pondered the subject as she took her place at the desk, to type the waiting letters.

Clunes called at the flat, the day following his broadcast. It was Sunday and Louella was free. She welcomed him, congratulating him on his performance of the previous night.

"They've offered me a short contract — I'll be in London for the next month."

She was filled with dismay as she realised what this would mean. "Does this mean that you are giving up your work in the north? Are you wise to throw up security . . . for this?"

"I'm banking all on this venture. There is much more money in it than in my own job. Why shouldn't I? We're only young once. I want to get money quickly. It's worth taking a risk — or two . . . " His healthy face was full of vitality. He was ten years younger than Eugene, she remembered. He expressed her own restless cry, she thought. They were all seeking something, experiencing the urge of youth.

When she did not answer he said carefully: "I'd be happy if only you and I could settle our differences. Why can't we, darling? It is all different now. You must see that for yourself. You love me, I'm sure you do, or I wouldn't persist like this." He leaned over the settee and put both hands tensely on her shoulders.

She sat motionless, feeling the heat of his hands, realising that he was willing her to respond. Her courage came to her aid and she shook off the restraining hands. "It wouldn't work out for us, Clunes."

He came round grimly, facing her

with suspicion in his manner. "Are you concealing something?"

"Yes, I suppose so. Eugene Charles, the author, asked me to marry him — and I will in a couple of weeks. You knew I was his secretary?" Her voice was uneven in spite of her resolution.

"Quick work." Clunes was taken aback, angry, abusive. "You can't know him; you haven't been in London long enough — or did you know him before coming? Is that it? Is he the real reason you came here?"

"No. I didn't know him before coming to London. You needn't take that line with me either. My mind is made up."

"Then — do you love him?" He sounded bewildered. He was both hurt and disappointed.

"What is love? Does it bring happiness? You don't have to be madly in love to get married. Lots manage without."

"Don't say that again." He caught her hands in a grip that made her cry out with pain. "Of course you need to be in love before you marry; that's what it's all about, you little fool. I wish I could fathom this situation. How can I reach you?" There was silence as he thought rapidly. "Will you marry him — without any feeling for him?"

"I like and respect him — isn't that enough?"

"No, it isn't. Not when it's you. He stands to gain, while you . . . oh, Lord . . . " He was glaring down at her angrily.

Suddenly he pulled her into his arms, holding her close.

"What's come over you, Louella? What changed you? I'm the fellow you love, darling. I love you. We were to be married. Nothing can change those facts. You still want me, don't you?"

She felt the physical appeal, and tried to move from his embrace. Contact undermined her resolution . . . made him more eager.

"You can't understand all that is involved. Nothing matters now save that I manage somehow to clear Wain's name. It isn't just myself any longer.

I'd do more than this if it would help Wain."

He shook his head. "Compensation? It doesn't make sense. If you believe Wain is innocent, then the case solves itself. You were never like this in the old days. I'm part of your life. You can't step into Eugene Charles' life and be happy. You and I belong — don't you see?"

She moved away from him, by sheer effort of will. Her face was white and strained. "You don't understand, Clunes. I'm sorry. I wish you hadn't come here. I wanted it to be over before you were drawn into it. When you insisted I had to tell you. I'm never marrying you and you know why."

He prowled up and down the room restlessly. "All right. So that's the way you feel? One day when life turns sour on you don't say you weren't warned. You're wrong and I wish I knew what set you this way. Are you sure this fellow will be kind to you?"

"I hope so." Reserve dropped over her, for she did not wish to discuss Eugene with him if she could avoid the issue.

"None of the motives you have given are a proper basis for marriage. How can you be happy?"

"Would marriage with you be any happier?" she flamed to life, turning on him so swiftly that he blinked. "Are you less selfish than he is? All men are selfish. If he demands a great deal at least he is willing to pay for it . . . " Too late she realised where the rash words had taken her.

Clunes stared at her as her face slowly whitened. "He's willing to pay? Do you realise just how bad that sounds?"

"You are deliberately provoking me. I wish you'd go. Do you hear? Go."

"All right — this needs thinking about."

He half turned, then on a sudden impulse he stepped back and caught her up against him, crushing her to his body. He kissed her full on the mouth and the savagery and strength of the kiss appalled her. She was almost fainting when he released her. She held on to the table, trying not to show how she felt.

"Can he make you feel that way?" Clunes asked in a shaken voice.

"You had no right . . . " she whispered.

"I wanted to remind you . . . you've no right to marry anyone but me. I won't stand for it. You must be mad. I've not finished yet. I'm coming back . . . " Anger was forcing him into the wrong, and his arms began flailing about as if he had no control over their movements. "I'm coming back, Louella . . . "

She turned her back, and heard him stamping out of the room, out of the flat, banging the outer door in a way that shook the building.

"Phew! I heard bits of that," Claribel confessed, as she came out of her bedroom. "I was getting kinda scared. He was in a little temper, wasn't he? You must have told him?"

"Yes, I did."

"Well, we can't all be wrong," Claribel pointed out.

Louella rushed to her room for her outdoor coat, and presently left the flat, feeling miserable and preoccupied. Why shouldn't she do what Clunes wished her to do? She was so actively unhappy that she did not know where to go. She passed a church, but could not bring herself to enter, although she listened wistfully to the singing. She thought of her father and Wain, and felt her throat constricting with pain. Why had life brought such misery to them all. Although she was advertising for Wain she began to question her own wisdom in doing so. Might she not be bringing fresh disaster and tragedy to them all?

"No," she whispered, white lipped. "I won't believe that. Wain is as innocent as I am. I have to believe." If she lost her belief in Wain she knew that life would not hold any meaning. The reason for being, for striving, would have gone.

She walked on, striving for calmness, too miserable to take account of time or direction. Was she being vindictive in not forgiving Clunes? Would she come to regret her attitude? Why was she so certain that he was wrong in his thinking? It was a certainty that arose out of inner conviction. Yet he had a right to his own convictions, as she had to hers. There was no chance of happiness for them while they both held firm. Better to be with Eugene, about whom she cared little, than to be torn with misery over Clunes, whom she loved.

Claribel thought she was wrong, but she could not judge because she was not in possession of the full circumstances. If only Clunes had not followed her to London. She sighed deeply as she walked along, hands deep in her pockets, shoulders hunched.

She entered Green Park, and almost at once saw Camille and the nurse. The child was playing happily with a ball on the grass, which needed cutting. Suddenly Louella felt happier. The child ran towards her, arms outstretched. Louella waited and swung her high in the air. Camille's sweetness was an antidote to her mounting misery.

"Again, Louella. Again." Louella swung her up again. "I'm glad you came. Did daddy tell you to come?"

"No, darling, I didn't know you were here. I — was just having a Sunday morning walk."

"Don't you mean a marathon?" Nurse said, smiling in a kindly way. "Camille — please don't do that." The child was clasping Louella round the knees, making progress impossible. They all laughed gaily.

"I don't mind. I love children," Louella felt much happier. There would be compensations. In trying to make Camille happier she would find her own contentment. She sat down on the grass, glad to rest.

"Tell me a story," Camille begged, the ball forgotten in the long grasses. She was full of imagination, with a quicksilver way of expressing herself. Louella forgot herself as she began to weave a story around Frieda and Freddie, the two ducks who had lived for years on one of the ponds near her home. "They're so old now — and so wise — that they do the strangest things." She explained for the benefit of the nurse, who had not heard the first instalment.

"An' they lived with Bluebell in a little caravan near the reeds ... " Camille prompted, settling herself happily into Louella's arms.

Nurse listened, too, as the story proceeded, with Frieda and Freddie taking the major roles. Camille gave small wriggles of delight during the next hour, until Louella's imagination came to a full stop.

"No more." Louella knelt up. "It must be nearly time for lunch."

"And I believe that is Mr. Charles' car," the nurse began to collect Camille's toys and coat. "Yes, here's your daddy, Camille."

The child raced across the grass to meet her father, and returned with him, hand in hand.

Nurse watched them. "He said he'd pick us up about one o'clock, and he's late."

Eugene smiled when he saw Louella. "I didn't know you were to be here, too?"

"Accidental. I was just walking — and saw Camille and nurse."

"Have lunch with us," he suggested easily.

"No, thank you. I'm returning home." Now that he was here she longed to get away, to end the embarrassment she felt in his presence. This was all the fault of a situation that was getting out of hand.

"Then I'll run you home." They all walked to his car, which was waiting at the entrance to the park. Camille climbed into the front seat beside her father, while the nurse and Louella sat in the rear seats. "I'll drop them at the house — then run you home. No trouble, I assure you. I'm glad to do it."

"Thank you." She wished that she had not met Eugene, and wondered miserably if he thought she had gone to the park with a purpose. She knew so little of what he really thought that she was filled with doubt and uneasiness. Had she indeed sought him unconsciously? The thought was so confusing that she coloured with embarrassment.

Camille clamoured for a longer ride, but Eugene was firm, and at the house he opened both doors, and saw the child with her nurse onto the pavement.

"Sit in front with me," he told Louella. When she had changed seats he started the car again, waiting for moments for several oncoming cars to pass before swinging out from the kerb.

"I could have taken a bus," she said.

"You have been kind in trying to gain Camille's confidence, in giving up part of your free time, and I appreciate that." He spoke almost absently, as if only part of his mind was answering her.

"But I didn't even know they were in the park. I was walking . . . "

He glanced at her straining hands, and then into her flushed face. "Something wrong?"

She told him about Clunes and the quarrel which had driven her from the flat. Words poured out of her, and she realised she was being indiscreet.

"If you really love him, we'd better call the whole thing off," he suggested grimly. "I wish you'd make up your mind."

"I have made up my mind — or at least, never changed it. Whatever Clunes says now I shall never marry him."

"Right. Then put it out of your mind."

"Men seem to find that kind of thing easier to do than women."

"Want me to deal with him?"

"No. I can manage him, but he takes some convincing."

"I expect he does." He smiled on the words, as if something amused him, and she was tortured with renewed doubts. This must all seem very trifling compared to the events in his full life. He drew up before the block of flats where she lived, and leaned over to open the car door. "Don't look so worried. It'll be all right. I wouldn't go on with it if I didn't think so."

"Even Claribel thinks it's — unorthodox. I'll be glad when we can settle down to a routine."

He gave her a puzzled look, saluted

her, slammed the car door, and moved back into the stream of traffic. Louella stared after him. His elusive quality was maddening, she thought.

The next two weeks sped quickly, an unreal quality in them that baffled Louella. On the morning of the wedding she realised that she did not know Eugene any better than she had when they first met. He was always charming, self-possessed, completely the unknown quantity. Almira Ashton drifted in and out of his life, certain of herself and her beauty in a way Louella could never be. She longed for even a part of the film star's poise.

Several days were given up to the fittings for her new wardrobe, and special care was taken over the dress which she was to wear on the evening of her wedding day. Eugene was paying for that and he insisted that it must be the best of its kind. She wondered why he was so insistent.

"Why?" he laughed easily when she asked him. "When you're paying over a hundred pounds for one dress you want it right, don't you?"

But she knew instinctively that was not the reason. As the hours to the ceremony grew less, she was too afraid to probe further for the real reason.

Claribel consented to accompany her to the ceremony, which would be quiet, with only two of Eugene's friends to act as witnesses.

"You'd have thought he'd want folks milling around," Claribel said disagreeably. "It would look more natural somehow."

"That comes later," Louella answered.

Claribel gave her a long, thoughtful look. "Well, if you're satisfied it's all right . . . at least it's a church wedding. I suppose one must be thankful for small mercies."

Her attitude softened as she helped Louella to dress for the ceremony. The wedding outfit was in ice blue, with white accessories. The colour suited Louella's dark hair. Her face was pale and wan for she had not slept properly for some nights.

"You look lovely," Claribel said, kissing her soundly. "I'm a confirmed old maid, and I know I've been sticking pins in you, but I won't any more. I'll pray that you'll find happiness — but just how beats me!"

Louella laughed in spite of herself. Clunes was away for the weekend and she had not told him the exact date of the wedding, so that she did not expect to see him for some days. Claribel promised that she would tell him the news as soon as she saw him.

"How you can resist that nice boy, I can't think."

Louella gave her a grave, preoccupied smile, not answering. There was so much more behind her decision than Claribel knew.

They went to the church in the car that Eugene sent for them. He was waiting, and turned quickly when they entered the church. Louella's agitation robbed her of reasoning power, and she stood tensely as the service proceeded that made her Eugene's wife. For better or for worse . . . She glanced at Claribel's impassive face, past her to the two friends of Eugene, feeling the emptiness of the building behind them.

Eugene took her hand, and led her to the vestry where she signed her name for the last time in the register. Eugene looked pleased, his strong face smiling and determined. His fair hair shone golden in the sunshine as they came up the aisle together. Louella felt him as a stranger, someone she might never know.

She was glad to see Claribel again. "Your gloves, dear. You forgot them. I'll see you at the hotel. Now what's going on?"

A small crowd had gathered round the gate, waiting to see who would emerge after the wedding. It was a famous church and many famous persons plighted their troth there. Louella passed them without seeing them, moving towards the parked car automatically.

"Well, that's over," Eugene said, when they were alone in the car, except for the chauffeur. He put one hand briefly over Louella's. "Has it been an ordeal?" He was brisk, unemotional, and she was glad of this. This would henceforth be her lot. They would abide by the strange bargain they had struck.

There were a dozen guests awaiting them at the hotel,all in gay mood. They were curious to meet Louella, and she tried to play her part as she moved among them. Claribel was in her element for she was an excellent mixer, and she mentally compared notes with her own menu for that evening, when Eugene was having an open house for all his friends.

"Sit near me," Louella whispered, feeling preoccupied and tired.

Claribel nodded, seeing the situation with all its dangerous undercurrents. Louella was swimming deep, almost out of her depth, but gallantly trying to find her way alone. She smiled at Claribel hazily, and began to chatter as if she were emerging from a dream.

"You look beautiful — and about as fragile as a piece of Dresden china,"

Claribel whispered. "Yet you've such a good appetite — I can't understand it."

Louella nodded and smiled. Her large hat was lying on a chair, and she appeared very young in the thin, blue silk dress. The meal passed over without incident, and it was during the toasts that Eugene's best man whispered something urgently to him.

"The press? Good. I hoped they would. Tell the boys I'll be out in five minutes. Better still — offer them all a drink." He turned to Louella. "How will you like to have your picture in the paper, Louella? It's a pity they can't take it in colour."

Claribel watched her colour faintly, and knew that this was all part of the plan. Eugene wanted publicity — now that the wedding was accomplished. The sooner the world knew, the better evidently.

Soon they all moved out into the foyer, where the reporters crowded round, apparently all asking questions at the same time. Louella stood silently at Eugene's side, the guests behind them while several pictures were taken. A flash bulb exploded, and there was a general laugh of derision. For ten minutes they lingered, Eugene and his two friends answering every question that was put to them. This was going to mean something to Almira Ashton.

Claribel excused herself hurriedly. "I have to fly, honey. I've done right by you — and if I don't go you'll be without your vitamins tonight. See you later."

Louella nodded and they separated. Already her luggage would have been taken to Eugene's house as she was not intending to return to the flat. Claribel could resume her bachelor girl existence, which Louella had interrupted so short a time ago.

The reporters took one last picture of them in the front of Eugene's magnificent car, for he had dismissed the chauffeur. "Honeymoon?" he was laughing and impatient to be away. "For a few days we are too busy for a honeymoon, but we're going to the Baltic later."

Louella knew the words had registered

and would appear in the account to be written up as soon as the reporter raced back to his office. Eugene swung the car out from the kerb, and it was all over. She felt nervous, full of strain, as she leaned far back and tried to relax. She had dreaded that Clunes might show up, in spite of knowing that he was out of town. So many things might have brought him back to try to stop the marriage to which he was so opposed. But it had passed without a hitch. She was foolish to live in fear. Clunes had accepted her decision, and now there was nothing that he could do. She tried not to think about Clunes, or indeed about anything in particular.

"It's over and you can rest this afternoon," Eugene said gently. "By the way, has your dress come for tonight?"

"Yes." Her eyes glowed suddenly. She was pleased with the dress that he had insisted on buying for her. She thought he would be surprised too when he saw her in the finished version. For his own reasons he had wished her to outshine every other woman in the room, during her first appearance as his wife. "It's — magnificent. I only hope I can live up to it."

"You will. You're looking beautiful today, Louella. I'd not realised just how beautiful until now. Yours is the quiet sort of beauty that grows on one."

She looked amused. "Thank you. A nice compliment and guaranteed to pep up my morale."

He shrugged. If he had expected her to be grateful he was disappointed. "Well, here we are. Just make yourself at home — and be happy. That's all I ask. I like people about me to be happy."

"Thank you." She followed him indoors, feeling the strangeness of the position.

Before he left her to go to his study, he said casually, "I've paid into your account two thousand pounds — you'll find the pass book on your desk."

Her cheeks burned as she thanked him. Instantly her thoughts were turned outward again as she thought of Wain and all she might now do for him. This money would provide the lever that would lift him out of the void into which he had sunk.

She went up the broad stairs to the room that was now to be hers. It was a large, pleasant room, with the usual bedroom furniture, and grouped about the open window, were two easy chairs, a small table, and several other things for her comfort. The carpet was new, close fitted in a soft blue, and she enjoyed the feeling that no person had any right here, save herself. This was to be her background and she had already planned several small alterations to suit her own personality.

For an hour she rested, trying to subdue the agitation in her mind. When she heard Claribel and her helpers arrive, she decided to go downstairs to welcome them. The cocktail party was to commence about seven o'clock and Claribel would need to work fast, she thought, smiling.

Claribel silently handed her two evening papers. Louella read the account of the wedding, and saw the pictures, which were very clear.

"All over town," Claribel commented, watching her. Louella left them on Eugene's desk, although he would probably buy his own. After seeing that Claribel was launched, with the freedom of the house, she returned to her room, knowing that the major part of this momentous day was still ahead of her.

She bathed and dressed carefully, brushing out her dark hair into shining waves. Last of all she slipped the gold lamé dress down over her head, adjusting the shoulder straps, studying her reflection in the long mirror. She wore shoes of the same material, and she glittered as she moved to survey herself critically. Across the breast soft blue velvet was folded which draped well against the gold lamé. Her small headdress was a skilful blending of the two materials and perched on her hair like a large butterfly.

Eugene knocked on the door and entered, standing for a moment, watching her. Their glances met.

"Well?" Louella asked.

He advanced towards her. "Completely beautiful . . ." he said gravely. He put his hands on her hips and turned her about. Her skin was fine and creamy against the rich, glittering gold of the material.

"Is it time?" she asked him, turning back. They both looked into the mirror. Eugene was distinguished-looking in evening dress, his fairness making him seem dashing and handsome.

He nodded, and his expression softened. "We'd better go down. You look exactly as I hoped you'd look."

She was without jewellery of any kind, for the gown was sophisticated enough without, and she had nothing that would be suitable. Her dark head was held proudly as she preceded Eugene from the room.

Camille hung over the banisters and Louella looked up.

The nurse tried to draw the child away, but she called to Louella excitedly.

"I'd forgotten. I promised to see Camille before going down. Excuse me." Louella ran up the flight of stairs, holding her gown in both hands. The child hung back, overcome with sudden shyness.

"You're a fairy princess," Camille whispered, open-mouthed with admiration.

Louella had not been thinking about Camille today, and a pang of dismay shot through her confusion of thought. Camille was dependent on her now for much of her happiness. She had overlooked so much in this complex situation. She knelt on the carpet and drew the child into her arms gently. They kissed each other with grave sweetness.

"Are you really my new mummy?" Camille asked.

"Yes. I suppose I must be, darling. Do forgive me for not coming up before, won't you? Nurse will you explain? It's been such an odd sort of day, and I'm sorry if I forgot . . . there was so much to do . . . " Her shyness and uncertainty did more for her than a bolder approach. Nurse had not been sure that she approved of this hurried marriage, but now she wondered if she and Sara had not been a little hard on the girl. She certainly did not seem to be in a hurry to interfere with existing arrangements.

"Why, of course. It's all been so sudden — don't crease that gown, Camille."

The child was stroking the material reverently. She looked straight into Louella's face. "When I grow up I'll have a gown just like this."

Louella realised that the gown had been created to excite comment. No one would guess how she felt at this moment before her ordeal. She stood up, drawing the child with her. "Darling, you shall. I'll see to it myself. There — you've smudged my lipstick, but it was worth it, wasn't it?" She let the child hold the hand mirror as she wiped her lips, and reapplied the lipstick which she carried in her small gold lamé bag. It was only then that she realised that Eugene had followed her. He stood just within the door, watching the scene critically. She

133

felt confused, caught out, for she had not known he was there. Quickly she put the lipstick away, and bidding both the child and nurse good night, hurried from the room.

Eugene followed her. "You're fond of the child, aren't you?"

"Yes. Who wouldn't be. She's a sweetheart."

The drawing-room looked magnificent, great bowls of flowers scenting the warm air. Claribel and her staff, were ready to bring in refreshments as they were needed. Already the first guests had arrived. Louella stood beside Eugene, acknowledging the introductions, trying to remember names and faces and failing utterly. It would be months before she sorted them all out, she thought. Eugene apparently knew everyone of importance in London, and she grew lost in the never-ending stream of names.

Hardest of all, was the veiled curiosity with which the guests regarded her. Even when they had moved away, she felt their critical eyes fixed upon her. The beauty of the gown she wore gave her moral support and she was soon so involved that she needed her full wits about her to cope with the situation.

The rooms buzzed with conversation and laughter. Louella grew more relaxed as she realised that the evening had got off to a good start. She began to wonder if she might be spared the ordeal for which this exquisite gown had been created. Surely Almira Ashton would not come now?

About nine o'clock Claribel drew close, and between half closed lips murmured: "Someone special arriving, my love. Remember the Boy Scouts."

Louella laughed. "You mean — be prepared?"

Eugene glanced round for her, and she moved instantly to his side. They were standing so, when Almira Ashton made her carefully timed entrance. She had left it until the room was full, and all the guests would be assembled. She swept forward with her escort, laughing and delightfully gay. Her beauty was in full flower and she held the gaze of everyone in the room.

She went straight to Eugene with both hands outstretched to take his. For a moment they looked into each other's eyes. "My dear Eugene — what a surprise for everyone. I simply had to come." Her warm, sweet voice brought silence to the room.

"I wanted you to come," Eugene said steadily. "Almira, you must meet my wife. Louella — Miss Ashton."

She turned to Louella with the same smiling gesture, but her eyes were cold. "I'm so delighted to meet you. May I call you Louella? What a charming, old fashioned name you have." Turning to Eugene again she murmured: "So this is your wife? Why, she's just a child, darling."

Louella felt the blue eyes appraising her whole appearance in a lightning glance. She was grateful now that she was wearing the golden gown. Exquisitely dressed as she was, Almira Ashton did not outshine her own appearance.

"I'm certainly not a child, Miss Ashton," Louella answered clearly.

Eugene repressed a smile. "I agree. You're just young . . . "

"Eugene and I have been friends for years — simply years, haven't we, darling? When I got your note this morning I was completely devastated, Eugene. I couldn't believe it — but now, having seen this sweet child, of course I can understand it all so much better." The purring voice slid over the situation with carefully prepared phrases. Almira Ashton was certainly not letting her world think she carried her heart on her sleeve. She was presenting a picture of old and tried friendship, one that would withstand all stress. The onlookers were clearly disappointed. They had expected an exhibition of temperament from the tempestuous Almira.

Only Louella was treated to the chill of her blue glance. Was this woman Eugene's discarded mistress?

Eugene stood with Almira's slim white hand in his, laughing, holding her reproachful gaze, explaining what had happened in a casual way that was disarming. Louella stood near him, listening. Weeks of preparation had gone into making this moment what it was, she thought. Was Eugene still in love with Almira? In spite of his wish, was his will power useless in her presence?

He drew Louella forward, and she knew that he wished her to join in the conversation. "Louella, you always wanted to meet Miss Ashton."

"Yes, I have," she acknowledged. "Until now, you have just been a voice over the telephone, Miss Ashton."

"Ah — of course — Eugene's secretary!" Almira half turned to the young man who was with her. "Lion, dear, do all great men marry their secretaries?"

"It ain't necessarily so . . . " Lion quoted, and there was a mischievous gleam in his sombre eyes. The words brought a laugh from the surrounding groups. Everyone appeared to be watching them, and Louella tried to meet the situation. The whole day had been a build-up for this moment when they three should meet. Eugene was ready, if Louella was not, and he kept the conversation from flagging. He seemed completely at ease.

Louella watched the beautiful woman, pondering how Eugene could resist her when he might so easily have married her. It was not logical. She was perfection, physically lovely from her ash blonde head to her shapely feet.

"I give up," Louella murmured, and coughed to cover the words.

Almira had heard her, however, and she turned towards her, smiling. The same thought was in both their minds apparently.

In a soft tone that did not reach further than Louella's ear she murmured: "You must know the answer? My husband refuses to divorce me — and as Eugene and I wish to remain — good friends . . . this is the only way . . . you understand?"

The innuendo nauseated Louella, and she suddenly felt cold and very frightened.

She doubted if Eugene heard the softly spoken words for his attention was temporarily withdrawn. She stood, looking into Almira's triumphant eyes, realising how she had become involved in a situation that could so easily end in tragedy. Eugene's marriage was not intended to be anything more than a shield behind which they could continue their association. The full meaning broke over her brutally and she knew it for truth.

Almira's lovely eyes were guileless when she saw that Louella believed her. She turned back to Eugene having shattered the girl's peace of mind. Very soon someone placed a glass in her hand and the conversation became more general.

Claribel came towards Louella. "Cheer up, darling. She's a viper. What'd she say to you? You know what to do with her type, don't you?" There was all the freedom of their old friendship behind the words.

"No. I — didn't . . ." A slow anger

was growing in Louella. She had trusted Eugene in spite of everything. She stood quietly, allowing herself to be absorbed in the babble of noise about her. Claribel came and went, the one rock of safety in the shifting sands of this new unstable life which she was entering. Dear Claribel, who had tried to warn her. Would she ever be happy again?

Ten minutes later Louella wished the evening safely over. She felt she could not bear what was surely about to happen. She saw Clunes enter the room, and heard the murmur of protest around him. He was swaying and had obviously been drinking heavily. One or two men tried to stop his progress towards Louella.

"Oh, no, you don't," Clunes shouted into the hubbub. "I've as much right here as any of you. Louella — tell your fine friends to leave me alone. Tell 'em . . ."

"Yes, please." Louella nodded to the men who released Clunes at once. To Eugene she said hurriedly: "It's Clunes and he . . . he . . ."

"He's looking for trouble," Eugene's eyes narrowed coldly.

"How simply fascinating," Almira Ashton was gazing at Clunes with open admiration. "I've always longed to have two men fighting over me — now they will soon be fighting — but over you, Louella."

The room was silent. Louella hoped she would not faint. Clunes straightened purposefully, and sneered at the two men who had sought to impede his progress. Louella knew that was not the way to control Clunes. In all his life he had not submitted to force and it would not do now. She hoped she would have some influence over him.

Forcing herself, she went towards him, speaking placatingly. "You were kind to come, Clunes."

Claribel was trying to help in the background, moving among the guests, offering distraction, urging them to further efforts in eating and drinking.

Clunes focused on her distressed face. "Louella — kind? What do you mean?"

"Come over here and sit down," she pleaded, taking his arm.

He shook her off angrily. "You're trying to get round me. You're too late — too late. But I'm not too late to tell that clot what sort of a wife he's got."

Eugene had followed her, and Louella raised a scared face to his in silent appeal. They sat down, hoping that Clunes would do likewise but he stood menacingly over them. Almira Ashton drew closer, agog for what must transpire.

"If you don't keep quiet I'll have you put out," Eugene threatened.

"I'll say what I've come to say."

"I think he should be allowed to speak," Almira murmured. "After all, it's a free country, isn't it?"

Clunes swept her an unsteady bow. "That's right, lady. It's a free country. I'm here to clear up a few misunderstandings. You think you've got a country mouse for a wife, don't you?"

"I'm not staying here to listen while you slander my wife," Eugene was so angry that he shouted the words.

Clunes pushed him down with one angry sweep of his arm. "You'll listen . . . "

"Please," Louella implored. She rose, determined to end the suspense one way or the other. "Come with me, Clunes — do you hear me?"

They measured looks and the drunken man allowed her to take his arm. He sneered at Eugene. "See? She's mine. Always has been. She belongs to me."

Eugene was white with temper but he allowed them to leave the room. The guests were stunned, the moment awkward, until Almira broke into a carefree laugh. She picked up a glass and handed it to Eugene.

"There, darling, have a drink. You need it."

Claribel signed to her assistants and they were soon circulating among the guests again. The tension slackened but the buzz of conversation that rose was concerned with the incident.

"Excuse me." Eugene drank deeply before replacing the glass on the tray. "I'll find Louella . . . "

3

"**O**F all the truly terrible insinuations to make about me," Louella spoke furiously, wringing her hands in nervous frustration. "I can't bear any more. You're hopeless and unkind . . ."

Clunes sat with his head buried deep between his hands, trying hard to regain sanity. He was so drunk that he was seeing even more clearly than usual. He was drunk, and miserable because of what he had done, yet with a satisfaction behind the surface mood that he had no wish to break into. Eugene's pleasure was spoiled, that was for certain. His jealousy led him on to break what he could not tolerate.

"You came here deliberately to break up the party," she said, hostility growing in her manner. "You don't know a thing about it but you act like a . . . "

"You know why I came here," he interrupted. "No use keeping on at me. Sure I'm drunk, but you get the truth from drunks and children."

Eugene entered the room closing the door after him. Louella was white, and her glance met his in desperation. Eugene watched them both for a moment, trying to gauge the truth.

"You'll either apologise to my wife — publicly, or I'll see my solicitors in the morning," Eugene spoke firmly, through set lips. His expression was far from pleasant.

Clunes sneered. "Don't you believe it's true?"

"No, I don't. You're acting like a jealous fool." He suddenly leaned down and peered into Clunes' flushed face. "Drunk, jealous, mad — which?"

"All three, I'd say," Louella said vexedly.

"Listen to me," Clunes spoke warningly, his words slurring over his thickened tongue. "You have to admit you were engaged to me — does he know about that?"

"Yes, I am aware that she was engaged to you."

Louella looked from one man to the other fearfully, feeling that she was gazing on a nightmare. Was there no end to the problem?

"So what?" Clunes sneered. "But for you we'd have been married. She wanted your money — didn't you know? She's not in love with you, brother. I could tell you plenty."

"That's enough. Either apologise or get out," Eugene ordered coldly.

Louella realised that they had only shifted the scene of battle after all. Clunes was not the type to apologise to any one. His recklessness might drive him in to even deeper indiscretion. What might he not reveal to Eugene, of Wain's disgrace, the family trouble? She felt unable to bear the revelations that she felt might be coming. It would have been wiser to tell Eugene herself. Clunes had nothing to lose — she was the one who would suffer deeply.

Unable to bear the scene another moment, she ran from the room, up the stairs to her own room. Clunes would tell Eugene everything and that would be the end. She had reached rock bottom.

Love? Was that what Clunes thought he felt for her? His jealousy stemmed from other emotions than love. Genuine love tried to comfort and help and build, not to drag down. She was aghast as she realised the implications behind his conduct. She had loved Clunes but his feeling for her must have been ineffectual. How near she had been to making a mistake, heading in to a lifetime of misery. She tried to bolster her shaken ego with this mounting anger, but felt the uselessness of the effort.

After an eternity Claribel tapped lightly on her door. "I'm not going away, Louella — let me in."

Louella unlocked the door.

"Why don't you come downstairs?

Clunes has gone. Eugene sent me to ask you to come down and finish the evening. I wish you would, Louella."

"They must all be talking — wondering . . . "

"They'll talk more and wonder more if you don't come. Eugene is carrying it off, and you should back him. He's in there now. The party is going well. You could circulate a bit, and let them see you again. That's all he asks."

"How can I — the way I look now?" Louella mourned over her excited appearance. Tears were still running down her face, her hair was dishevelled.

"We'll soon fix that — if you're willing?" Claribel smiled into the woebegone face.

"Does everyone believe what Clunes said about me?"

"I don't — Eugene doesn't — why trouble about the others?"

"But I do . . . in a way," Louella began to cheer up when she realised that she had their support.

"That's better. This isn't the end of the world."

"It felt like it for a while. I don't really want to meet those strangers again."

"Those strangers are Eugene's friends — they may be yours one day. Who knows?" Claribel spoke with emphasis. "This will pass. Eugene insists that you come down and I feel he's right." She handed Louella the sponge and towel, with a gentle smile. Finally Louella powdered and renewed the lipstick, glancing in the mirror wonderingly. Her gown and general appearance showed none of the fury of despair that had racked her.

"You're lovely," Claribel comforted. "Quite normal again and no one will guess if you carry it off jauntily. Eugene will — you'll see."

They went down the stairs together, and for some minutes Claribel stood chatting to Louella, as if consulting her on some point of catering. They stood within the door, feeling the curious glances that were directed on them. Eugene's restless gaze found them at once and he hurried forward, after excusing himself to his friend. The strain eased on his handsome face as he drew Louella further into the room.

"There you are, dear. I'm sorry about what occurred just now. The fellow apologised and left. He'll send you a written apology when he sobers up. Discarded boy friends are the limit, aren't they?" He was speaking clearly and several guests standing nearby must have heard him. His backing amazed Louella, heartening her considerably. If he could rise to the occasion like this then she must try . . . but of course he didn't really care about anything but his own prestige. The thought was more bitter than anything yet. Once more she was drawn into the throng, joining in the laughter and talk, even able to discuss what had happened in a light, flippant way.

"Poor dear man," Almira Ashton was never far from Eugene. "It must have been a shock when he barged in here — claiming all sorts of horrible things." Louella thought this was odd, considering the stories that circulated about Almira.

Eugene laughed reminiscently. "It rather misfired, didn't it? Clunes is no stranger to me. However, let's talk about something more interesting. Louella, you must have something to eat."

He was determined that outwardly at least, he would save the situation, she thought miserably. The strain on Louella was terrific but she welcomed the duties that awaited her, until presently they were bidding farewell to the last of the guests.

Claribel and her helpers were finishing in the kitchen, which Sara had handed over to them for the evening.

"All these things will be called for in the morning," Claribel told Louella, yawning as she packed and sorted. "Don't look so worried, my love. Nothing is ever as bad as it seems."

"Didn't everything go off well — apart from — that . . . ?"

"Yes. Now I'm off too. Have a rest . . . you look to need one. I'll see you tomorrow." Claribel bustled off, not staying to probe further. She was disturbed but not even to herself would she admit that Louella's life was in ruins. She needed time to think about that before she could pronounce judgment. "Hell bent — that's Clunes . . . poor chap."

Louella closed the door on her reluctantly. "Good night." She went to the drawing-room, and then to Eugene's private den where he was taking a drink, thoughtfully swishing the liquid around in his glass. He glanced up as he felt her presence there. There was no smile between them.

"I'm just going," Louella said. "Good night. I'm sorry — about everything."

"Wait. I want to talk to you." He went to the door and closed it, so that they were in a small oasis of silence, the slowing down sounds in the house shut out. His eyes were fixed on her perturbed face as he said, "Your friend Clunes . . . "

"I'm very sorry he caused such a disturbance . . . " Her voice shook.

"So am I. I'd just like your reassurance that none of what he said was true."

"Then you only pretended to believe . . . do you think it is true?"

"I don't know what to think. I feel he was bent on mischief, but I'd appreciate it now if you'd give me a straight denial."

She tried to subdue her agitation. "I do deny his insinuations. We were engaged — I told you that, but I've never been his mistress if that is what you are thinking. I did love him and I thought he loved me but after tonight I could never believe that he did."

"Why didn't you marry him?"

The question was one she dreaded. "We — disagreed . . . "

"On what, if I may ask?" Seeing her mutinous expression he added: "I realised how you feel, but you must remember that I have a right to know the reason for — many things."

The reminder hurt her, but she tried to be fair. "I can't tell you any more. It was jealousy that made Clunes talk the way he did tonight. He's been making me miserable for days, trying to change my mind, but he couldn't." She recalled Clunes' words when he inferred that she married Eugene for his wealth and position, and her cheeks burned. "Do you mind if we leave this until morning?"

He seemed to debate the situation silently. "All right. The fellow promised to write an apology. We'll talk about it when we hear from him. Good night, Louella."

The battle was over, and she was too thankful to probe into his reaction. She left him, running up the stairs to her room, where she locked the door. Throwing herself across the bed, she cried bitterly, giving way to the tempest of tears that had threatened all evening. Life had been difficult enough, without this final insult, she thought.

When Clunes came to his senses he would probably be horrified, too. She hoped earnestly that he would, for he deserved to suffer, too, and she would jog his memory if necessary.

Morning brought a degree of calmness, after a sleepless night. Louella was at the breakfast table at the usual time, but Eugene had already eaten, and gone out. She wondered if he meant to avoid her.

At eleven o'clock Clunes rang the doorbell and was admitted. Louella agreed to see him because it was the lesser of two evils. He looked dissipated in the brisk morning light, and obviously had a headache.

"I had to come," Clunes said when she appeared. "Do you mind?"

"Leave your hat on the table, and come in here," Louella led the way into the office, where she was accustomed to working. It was the only room on the ground floor where she felt to be at ease. She sat down at her desk, and motioned Clunes to take a chair by the window. "Eugene is out. Wouldn't what you have to say wait until he returns?"

"No. I don't care a damn what he thinks. It's you, Louella. I have to try to square myself with you. I'm wretched about last night. There's no excuse; I'd been brooding and drinking for hours." He ran a nervous hand over his smooth, dark hair, his gaze seeking hers anxiously.

"You thought that by blackening my character that might help?" she asked sarcastically.

"I'm sorry . . . "

"Frankly, if it had been true I couldn't have felt more grieved — but to deliberately concoct such a lie — well, Clunes, I'm speechless." Her coldness stung him into speech.

"I wish it had been true. I wish I had some hold over you. How you can marry a man you don't even like . . . "

"You are mistaken. I do like Eugene. I like and respect him. I'd certainly not have married him if I hadn't. I'm not so muddled that I can't think straight. I hope he feels the same way about me, but since you tried to smear my character so deliberately it's made me scared. I'm proud that he took the stand he did, and didn't just let it drift. It's up to you to repair the damage if you can. Everyone knows you were drunk but it doesn't excuse you completely. I told you that you'd get into serious trouble one day if you wouldn't stop drinking."

"Now I have, eh?" Clunes shrank from the bitterness in her tone. "Nothing you can say is as bad as the way I feel. I love you, Louella."

"I wonder. A lot of what you feel is self-pity. How do you suppose I feel? It's not funny to be the talk of the town. Almira Ashton will see to it that it gets around, if no one else does."

"You know what everyone says about her and Eugene? She's no room to talk — neither has he!"

Louella eyed him frostily. She was wearing a jumper and skirt and looked cool in the lilac shade. "I refuse to discuss the situation with you or anyone else."

"Afraid of what you might unearth? I agree, it may be as well to let sleeping dogs lie."

Her anger was growing. "That's unworthy of you. You'd better go." She got to her feet, determined to end the interview.

He strode behind her, turning her about with sudden savagery. "You are very high and mighty all at once. You can't treat me as if I were a stranger. What's happened to us? This can't have changed you . . . "

She looked at him blankly. "No, this hasn't changed me. It was before . . . yet I didn't know."

"What do you mean?" he asked sharply. "What do you mean, Louella?"

"I don't know. The feeling must have been there all the time — before I left home, I mean . . . was that partly *why* I left home?" Their eyes met in hostility.

His hands dug into her shoulders angrily. "Listen to me . . . "

"Take your hands off me."

She was frightened in spite of her calmness. This was not fun to Clunes, or to herself. She felt the emotion and confusion under which they were both labouring. His hands were hot, his eyes bloodshot and wild. He tried to draw her closer with a strength she could not deny.

"Leave me alone, Clunes."

He swept her close, holding her, his face against hers. He groaned deeply. "You little fool, you don't know what you're saying — what you've done. You love me."

She tried to free herself but he would not be denied. She began to tremble and knew that she could not resist him for long. Suddenly the fight went out of her and she relaxed against him.

"Don't you?" he breathed. "Say it."

She nodded against him. Yes, she had loved Clunes for years and the feeling was not one she could put aside. She was frightened of the primitive emotion her admission unleashed between them.

"Say it," he insisted.

"Yes — I love you. Oh, let me go. If you love me, let me go." Her voice was unsteady. She must get away from him. If she had realised the feeling between them as clearly as this, she would never have married Eugene. All misunderstanding and bitterness faded beneath the love they had for one another.

Clunes slackened his hold, and she wondered that he could subdue his emotion so quickly. "I love you, darling — in spite of what you've done. You must leave Eugene at once. He can't expect you to stay now."

"But he knew all about you before, and he still . . . no, let me think. You must give me time."

"Time is never the essence of an agreement. Are you already his wife?"

She knew what he meant. "No. Not in that sense."

"Are you coming away with me?"

"No." The world might be swaying but she knew that was not the answer. She had made a bargain with Eugene and must honour it. "I can't. There must be some other way. Please leave me now, Clunes."

"With so much unsaid?" He clenched his hands and put them in his pocket. "Set a date when I can come again, and I'll live for that."

"Two weeks today," she said presently. "Please don't come before because there

161

is so much to plan. I'll try to think of a solution, honestly I will. Eugene trusts me and I must have time . . . "

Clunes put a hand to his forehead and it came away damp. "Blast. What a mess we're in. You'll plan something — for us?"

"I promise." She evaded him, taking her stand by the door.

As he passed her his eyes were on her lips. "Until next week then."

"Two weeks today," she reminded him steadily.

He left her, and she waited until she heard the outer door close on him. Only then did she relax her vigilance. She sat down in an armchair, her face ashen. Clunes had left her no loophole, and she was frightened by his veiled dominance over her.

There was not time to collect herself before the small door at the far end of the office opened and Eugene appeared. She watched with fascinated eyes as he lounged casually into the room.

"I heard most of that conversation,

Louella. At first I wasn't listening, then found I couldn't avoid doing so. Better for you to know."

"I — thought you were out."

"I was until half an hour ago. I meant to join you and Clunes but — the opportune moment didn't arrive."

She tried to defy his probing look. "Then you would hear the truth — that we still love each other?"

"Yes — and I'm glad to know there was no truth in his previous insinuations."

The coldness of his tone made her eyes flash with resentment. She could scarcely recall just what Clunes had said. She was too overcome to argue with Eugene, and she hurried from the room. Could anything have been worse than to know that Eugene had overheard every word?

In her room she tried to control her racing nerves. Life had to go on, the situation was not materially changed, although she knew herself more than she had previously. Clunes had forced her to admit that she still cared for him, and only in his arms had she allowed herself to believe this. Until now she had been able to subdue her natural feelings.

She lay thinking until it occurred to her that she had certain duties, that her life had now to be lived round the situation she had created. For an hour she played with Camille, giving the nurse a little freedom, and later, feeling considerably calmer she went down to Eugene's office and typed some letters that she knew awaited attention. Eugene spent four hours of every day at his desk, never allowing the busy life he lived to encroach on his working life.

He stood up when she entered. His glance was keen and searching and she tried to meet it. "Are you feeling better now?"

"Yes, thank you. I'd promised to type your letters so here I am."

"Thank you. It isn't worth while getting a secretary until after we've had that holiday."

164

"Gotland?" She turned to him in relief. "Is it still on?"

"Yes, but not for another couple of days, so we can take our time. I'm finishing an article, so perhaps you could type that later too?"

"Yes, of course." The routine helped, the work soothed her racing nerves. It was soothing to sit in here with Eugene, while he smoked and worked quietly. There was never any fuss about what he did. Always it was accomplished with a minimum of trouble. He knew what he wished to say and said it, leaving the finished word as proof of his efficiency. It must be wonderful to be so efficient, she thought. In spite of herself she became absorbed in the highly technical article. When the letters were signed she slipped out to post them.

On her return Eugene said: "Thank you, Louella. Not only for this, but for holding to our bargain when Clunes was here. I realise it must have been difficult. I hope you won't do anything decisive without first letting me know."

His calmness helped her. "I — promise," she whispered.

"Good. Well, don't slave down here indefinitely. It isn't necessary. Do you want me to take you out anywhere?"

This was said as an afterthought, for obviously he had his own plans.

"No, thank you. Will you be out all evening?"

"Yes." He did not tell her where he was going. Would he be with Almira Ashton? The thought burned in her mind and suddenly she was very angry. He expected her to honour their bargain yet he was carrying on an intrigue beneath the cloak of an apparently respectable marriage. She felt bewildered beneath the force of her sudden anger. Where did right begin and end? How was one to know what was right, and what was wrong? He had no right to judge her conduct in the light of his own.

She heard him leave the house later. She went upstairs to play with Camille, finding comfort with the child until it was her bedtime. Camille was growing to love her, and enjoyed the endless stories she was creating for her benefit.

The following morning when they were having breakfast together, Eugene threw down a challenge which she could not ignore. She was appalled by the sudden tension that swept between them at his abrupt words. She had come down a little earlier than usual, feeling that she must take up her household duties some time. Eugene acknowledged her quietly but continued going through his mail before drinking the coffee which she poured for him.

"Thank you, Louella."

Sara brought in his plate of bacon and egg, with toast for Louella. She settled quietly behind the coffee pot, busy with her own thoughts, glad that he was apparently employed. He looked up, catching her gaze deliberately.

"I'm definitely going to Gotland. Are you coming with me?"

She was shaken by his brusque demand. "Do you wish me to?"

"Yes. I'm not going alone." His words

held a hard ring and she wondered if he had resented her hesitation.

"What about Camille — the house?"

"They managed before you took over."

"Is that quite fair?" she asked, meeting his gaze.

"Is it fair to put obstacles in the way as you do?"

The question surprised her, and she tried to be honest in her thinking. "If you feel this way about it, of course I'll go." It would be a relief in one way, she thought, and a change, too . . . "When do you want me to be ready?"

He looked surprised. "I'll ring the agents in a few minutes and get particulars. We go by train and boat — not flying. It takes longer but is such a pleasant journey that I like it better. Two nights and a day probably. You *want* to come, don't you?"

She evaded the question. "I've never been to Sweden or the Baltic."

"I was there when I was writing the book. You'll like the island I fancy. The roses will be out too and that's quite something. Ruins and roses . . . and scent . . . and antiquity . . . quite an atmosphere." He smiled as he spoke, and she wondered what lay behind his manner.

"I should read your book before going perhaps?"

"I wouldn't bother. Make your own deductions and read it later — maybe. That way you could find out, if you agree with my findings on the subject."

"Which subject?" She felt to be getting out of her depth again but wanted to keep him talking. The tension was leaving him now that she had capitulated so easily.

"Love . . . " he said teasingly.

"Do you ever write a book without love in it somewhere?"

"Would it be more interesting without?" His eyes met hers across the table. "I don't think so, anyway."

"You didn't answer my question."

"Neither did you. Well — since you ask . . . I believe a novel has to be like life, with both sides of life shown up for completeness." It was said so smoothly that she bit her lips nervously. He would not fence with her. "So? No comment?"

She was unable to answer, for she knew that he had spoken with *double entendre*. It was not the first time that she had felt the granite smoothness beneath his casual manner. She rose to her feet. "I'll go upstairs now. Camille was dressed and wanted me to read to her while nurse was busy. I think I promised . . . "

Eugene strode round the table, and put a hand out to stop her flight. "Just a minute. You *want* to come with me, don't you? This isn't some form of penance — because you feel you owe me something?"

"I want to come if . . . " She could not finish the sentence and he saw her distress. He scrutinised her flushed face deliberately before he answered.

"If I'll behave myself? I don't intend being a nuisance, Louella, but I warn you . . . I'll look after my own interests. I'd like to enjoy this break. It's two years since I had a holiday — away from work, with a girl. Let's have fun for a few days, and forget our troubles — shall we?"

"I'd love it," she agreed, for the idea appealed to her.

"Then you'd better start packing for we may leave this evening. I'll let you know when I've contacted the agents. See you later." He released her and she turned away thankfully. He understood her better than she understood herself, and she was grateful to him. She hurried up the second flight of stairs to Camille's room, and presently settled down with a contented little girl on her knee. The day might be dark, with rain falling heavily, but the little girl was content to have her attention.

Louella began to prepare her for their absence. "We won't be away long. It's a wonderful place, with an ancient wall round the town and medieval buildings, all tumbling down. Lots of roses, too, your daddy says." Her words brought a sense of unreality and inner excitement. It would be wonderful to have an escort like Eugene on such a trip. Her thoughts stopped and she could not envisage the reality.

Presently Eugene bounded up the second flight of stairs. "Hullo, Camille. How's my darling this morning?"

The child rushed into his arms. She wanted to be included in the coming holiday, and she was hard to resist.

"No, sweetheart. We can't take you this time — but we'll plan a real holiday soon. We're leaving this evening, Louella, so will you be ready by about four o'clock? We'll board the boat tonight."

Louella was already leaving the room. "I'll be ready." She hoped that Eugene would be able to make peace with Camille for she was disappointed. They did not meet again until Louella stood waiting, with her case packed, about four o'clock. She was dressed in a neat grey costume, with white accessories, a travelling coat in grey tweed over one arm. She had earlier rung Claribel, but as she was out, had asked for a message to be given to her later. Claribel might feel hurt if she were not told of the changed plans. In any case it would only be a long weekend away from home.

A taxi came to the door, Camille ran down the stairs to bid them farewell, Eugene slipped into his mackintosh.

"Bring me a present," Camille whispered to Louella.

"I promise, darling," Louella hugged the little girl, feeling the familiar tenderness that was growing stronger between them. "I'll not forget."

Eugene held the door open, and she went out, waving as long as she could see the small figure of the child. Excitement rose in a heady wave as she entered the taxi. This was different from the way she had thought it would be. Life was carrying her onward, to broader horizons, and she tried to meet the challenge.

"Pity it's still raining," Eugene said. He looked handsome, clean shaven, very alert. They flew to Scotland, where they would embark by boat for Sweden. From that moment she felt to move in a dream world. There was no longer any substance to the things she did. She boarded the boat in the darkness, feeling the damp night air, the moon rising behind the rain clouds. The chug of the waves was heavy against the boat sides, against the dock, utterly dark and suggesting — depth. They went down into the cabins, which were next to each other.

"Yours, ma'am." The steward smiled at her as she moved past him.

I hope I'm a good sailor, she thought, knowing she would find out that night.

Eugene turned aside to his own cabin, and the steward presently left them. Louella glanced about her, seeing the open port hole, with the damp air coming in clear and chill. They were to sail with the tide. While she was still undecided how much to unpack, Eugene knocked on the cabin door and opened it. He smiled when he saw her standing in the middle of the cabin. The sounds of the bustle of departure were sharper now. There was an urgency gathering beneath the heavy tread on deck, the engines were throbbing to life.

"Are you all right in here, Louella?" He glanced round casually.

"Yes, thank you. Are you sharing your cabin?"

"Yes — a young Swede. Nice chap. Do you want to go on deck before turning in?" He was still in his mackintosh and looked very wide awake.

She hesitated, glancing at her wrist watch. It would be wiser not to go. "It's after ten — and so dark. We wouldn't see much. Do you mind if I don't?"

He laughed as if her hesitation amused him considerably. "Yes, I do mind. Put your coat on again and come with me. We want to see what we can, and you need fresh air before you sleep. I won't eat you." He laughed again.

She pulled on the travelling coat and caught up her handbag. "Lead the way. I'm rather glad you insist."

He led her up on deck, and when they gained the side they felt the ship was already in motion. The coils of rope were being wound into place, the shore appearing to recede as the gap widened between land and boat. The push of the sea — was stronger with every reverberation of the engines. Louella thrilled to the unfamiliar sounds, and drew in long breaths of the fresh ozone, the smell of seaweed, of tarred rope and wet decks. They picked their way along the deck, the receding shoreline a blur of lights on the horizon. The breeze freshened, and she felt the unsteadiness of the boards beneath her feet. She reeled as a long wave struck the ship.

Eugene took her arm to steady her. "You haven't got your sea legs yet, Louella." She realised that he was enjoying the experience and surmised that he was probably a good sailor. Men usually were. He drew her closer as they walked up and down, among the few people who had also come on deck to see the last of the homeland. The ship was settling down to the voyage. A chill wind swept them and Louella shivered. Eugene felt the movement. "Feeling cold?" he murmured, protecting her as well as he could.

"Yes. Perhaps I should go down now."

"Can I get you a drink or anything?"

"No, thank you." They had dined earlier. "I feel it will be wise to get to bed and to sleep as quickly as possible. I hope I'm a good sailor. How can one be sure?"

He laughed gently at her anxiety. "One can't. You'll soon know. It's not often I'm affected but occasionally I feel grim in a real storm. If you do feel sick, don't fight it. Just let it rip. Knock on the wall if you need help."

"Thank you." She spoke so dubiously that they both smiled. She held out her hand when they reached the cabin. "Thank you for everything, Eugene. You are very kind."

He sighed with considerable feeling. "I could be a whole lot kinder if only you'd let me."

She pushed the door open behind her. "Goodnight."

"Goodnight." He went off whistling,

slightly out of tune, but he appeared to be in a good frame of mind.

They met at breakfast. "I'm a good sailor . . . " Louella told him.

"Not even a headache?" His eyes were amused.

She shook her head and enjoyed the meal he ordered. Presently they went on deck, where they sat wrapped in rugs in a couple of deck chairs during most of the morning.

Great waves piled up against the horizon, which continued grey and chill, but Louella, sheltered in her corner, found a wonderful sense of freedom and peace. Eugene was proving to be a charming companion, and she knew that he was deliberately trying to interest her. He kept the conversation away from personalities, until she relaxed and began to enjoy herself.

She studied him when she could without attracting his attention, wondering how far one might trust such a man. He was very handsome, his profile strong, the blue eyes dominating his brown face.

Was she right to distrust such a swift emotion as he had professed to feel? He had said the attraction between them was there from the first moment, but she was very far from sure that this was the case.

They arrived the following morning, later crossing to Gotland by ferry. The scene was like the slow unwinding of a film, she thought, as they hung over the dock side. Eugene was taking colour film, absorbed in the fairylike approach to the island, which was enchanting in the strong sunlight. The ruins of the buildings as they drew closer, looked like teeth, then like benevolent monsters, changing every moment in contour. The well-preserved wall that surrounded Visby was clearly outlined, and Louella experienced again the awakening surge of excitement that she had lost in the lethargy on board ship.

The bustle of arrival, the overall silence that even their entrance could not wholly break, the business of finding their hotel outside the town, their rooms in that hotel, were all part of the unreality. She felt that she would surely hear the whirr of cameras and someone would yell "Cut" . . . and — life would begin again.

She stood alone in the spotless bedroom trying to believe that she was here. The hotel was modern, with every amenity, even a swimming pool. Eugene had been right, there was an atmosphere here.

She took time over dressing, enjoying the feeling of being static again. Presently they went down to dinner. Louella had changed into a summer frock and felt refreshed and very hungry.

"I've got the oddest feeling," she told Eugene shyly. "I feel as if I've been here before."

He glanced up from the menu. "Have you got it too? It's the durndest feeling, isn't it? I had it once, but having spent a couple of months here I've lost it now and can't trust the feeling any longer. Do you recognise anything specifically?"

She shook her head. "Oh, no. It's just a general feeling that I've seen it all before. Perhaps it's because you told me about your novel? You described it so graphically — that must be it." She pushed back her dark hair carelessly, surveying the other guests in the long room. It was a pleasant place, quiet and orderly, utterly relaxing.

They ate the excellent meal that was placed before them. It was pleasant being with such a man as Eugene, she thought secretly. After the meal they walked in the garden, enjoying the late evening sunshine. Eugene held her attention as he related part of the island's history, for he had read extensively before writing his own novel.

Suddenly Louella stopped, laughing at herself, unable to keep pace with her awakening perception and uneasiness. "This is the oddest feeling. Every word you say adds to it too . . . I'm quite sure I know what is round that corner. Yet, I've never been before. I can't have been here before."

He stood in front of her, his eyes watchful, his manner restrained. "Tell me — what is round the corner, Louella? You could be right. If you are wrong it doesn't matter. We can explore together."

"There's a pond or artifical water of some kind . . . a bridge over it. In the background are hundreds of rose bushes. There's a little summer house, too, but not the kind we have in England. It's smothered in roses. There are seats grouped about the pond . . . It's quite enchanting." He took her hand, hurrying her along the path. "Let's go see . . . "

She was experiencing his sense of hurry when they reached the end of the path, and could see ahead into the darkening garden. As they rounded the great cluster of bushes he drew her close to his side. In the distance they could see the shimmer of water beneath a faint moon, rising slowly and majestically in a luminous sky. Across the water lay a dilapidated wooden bridge, and beyond it a building surrounded by roses.

Louella drew in a breath of the fragant air. She was ashamed of her emotion. "It doesn't make sense. I must have been here as a child — yet I would never have forgotten. How could anyone forget such beauty? Yet I couldn't have imagined it either."

"I wouldn't know." There was a strained note in his voice. "Let's go nearer."

"I don't want to. It may be bewitched." She hung back dubiously.

"There might be something here — for us," he urged.

She went because he would not be denied. They did not cross the bridge for it looked too unsafe, but it was easy to walk round the pond to the summer house. The heavy scent of roses was strong about them, petals strewed the track in profusion.

"Like walking into fairyland," Louella said.

"I never found the magic when I was here on my own," he said gently. He drew her into the shadowy building. "Let's not be sensible, Louella. Let's give the magic a chance. I'm a believer in magic — didn't you know?"

"There's a lot I don't know about you."

She pushed back the stole she was wearing, feeling a sudden warmth in this enervating place.

"You could learn," he suggested . . . "if you wanted to. Do you?"

"I don't know." She was troubled, trying to be sensible for both their sakes. The moon was climbing higher, casting an intense light over their hiding place, illumining the scene before them to wondrous beauty. The hotel was like a palace in the skies, glistening with light, the sky a backdrop, almost purple where stars peeped through. Louella felt unsteady as she gazed bemused upon the scene.

Eugene stood with one arm about her shoulders. He was silent for some time too, seeming to find it hard to break the pressure of silence.

"I wanted to bring you to this island, so that we'd get to know each other, so that you'd learn to trust me, Louella."

"I do trust you," she whispered.

"One day when we're happier we'll come again, but I want you to know this, while we're away from our workaday selves. I want our life together to bring us both great happiness. I don't know how we'll achieve this but I'm willing to wait — and to work to attain what I want. In you I feel that there is the promise I seek. Somewhere between us is the feeling that I want more than anything else on earth."

His low voice came thoughtfully, with utter sincerity, and she listened with her heart. Was he right? Before they could attain what he wished there was so much to make right, to understand. Was the fault on her side — because she could not be sure?

"We might cut through the differences — take a short cut — but I'm not sure that is the way for us," he resumed gently. "You've been hurt and I've no wish to hurt you further. One day you'll understand."

In that moment of earnestness they were closer than they had ever been.

185

She tried to move away from his encircling arm, but he would not allow it. She was trembling with indefinable feeling.

"Please — I can't bear any more, Eugene." He must know that this was what she had hoped to avoid, yet she could not regret his declaration. It was as frank as she had known his nature to be.

He sighed. "Well — tell me, is this the scene as you imagined it?"

She nodded, almost afraid to admit even to herself how close the reality came to her imagination. "Yes, very like."

"It's all wrapped up with the pull the island had for me a year ago. Louella — if I asked you . . . " His hand was suddenly hard on her shoulder.

"No." She was stiff-lipped with sudden tension. Twisting from beneath his arm she ran out of the summer house, across the purpling sward towards the hotel. She was safely back on the path before he caught up with her.

"You can run; don't you know that you'd no need to?"

In silence they walked up the steps to the hotel. She had told him that she trusted him, yet her flight had proved otherwise.

"I'm sorry . . . " she whispered.

His eyes were cold, all warmth gone from between them. "That's all right. Goodnight. I hope you sleep well."

"Thank you." She sped up to her room on the first floor, not glancing back. The past hour had tried her strength more than she realised.

It was almost an hour later as she lay with her hands clasped behind her head, that she began to laugh, soft laughter that welled up from a relieved heart. Eugene must think her temperamental. Tomorrow she would do better. She liked him, that was for sure, and she knew now that he liked her. She was intrigued as she wondered what he had been going to ask her in the summer house.

She managed to ask him the following day when they were driving along the dusty road. The sun was overpoweringly hot, the scent of roses intoxicating.

"You really want the answer?" he asked, in lazy amusement.

"Yes — I think so."

"I'll tell you this evening — in the summer house."

"Tell me now. I'm curious."

"I'm not in the mood. By the way, you look pretty today, Louella. I like you in that colour. You should wear it all the time."

"Ice blue?" She looked down at the sleeveless dress she was wearing.

He touched the skirt, feeling the texture. "Silk, isn't it?"

She wore white gloves, handbag and straw hat, with dark glasses to guard her eyes from the fierce light. The morning had been spent on the beach, lazing, reading or talking as the mood took them. The past was past, and in this place where time appeared to stand still, she almost forgot the unhappiness of the last few months. She lived so intensely in the present that she had to make a conscious effort to recall any life before this one. Yet waiting behind the curtain that closed the past to her, was the biting pain of memory. Deliberately she circumvented the mood that would rob her of this new found peace.

Out of a long silence she said: "We must buy Camille a present."

"We must — or we needn't return home. Let's go to the shops now and choose something suitable." They left the car and wandered freely among the shops, commenting on all they saw. They bought an expensive toy for Camille, a handbag for nurse, a scarf for Sara.

"I'd like something for Claribel," Louella said. Her eyes flashed when she saw the bracelet. "The very thing; she likes chunky jewellery. Is it terrifically expensive?"

"No. I'll get it for you."

"I have money of my own," she remonstrated. While they were in the shop Eugene pointed to a stand nearby bearing necklaces.

"Do you like those?"

"Yes, but the bracelet will suit her better."

"I wasn't thinking of Claribel. I'll buy you a necklace if you'll choose the one you prefer."

Her eyes met his mutinously. "No."

"Yes." His mouth shut in a determined line.

"I'd much sooner you didn't. I don't want you to buy me a present."

Eugene ignored the request, and the attendant brought and displayed the necklaces. Louella watched while Eugene selected one. "This one?"

She smiled and nodded, seeing that to refuse further would embarrass him. Presently with their various packages they returned to the car.

After dinner that evening, he took her arm. "Come on, we're going back to fairyland."

She was in a reckless mood, and she went unhesitatingly where he led. She almost expected to find that the pond and bridge and summer house had vanished, but they were still there.

He waited for her to step with him onto the purple sward. The night was soft and benign, the intense heat of the day withdrawn, leaving only a gentle breeze to fan the parched earth. There was not even the cheep of a bird, the rustle of a leaf, the sound of a footfall, as they walked softly towards the summer house, shrouded in its shadows.

"It's like stepping back a thousand years . . . " she whispered.

"I'd an idea things might have changed, but they haven't."

She laughed in excitement. "I thought last night only happened once in a lifetime."

"It's something that will stay with us all our lives. Do you like this trinket, Louella?"

He held out the necklace on one finger, gently moving it back and forth to catch the rays of the moon. She put out her hand, but he held it away teasingiy.

"If you like it I'll put it on for you." He moved behind her at her slight nod, and placed the gleaming necklace about her throat, taking his time over the fastening. She was dreamily content as she felt the chill of the pendant against her warm skin. For a moment there was silence.

Eugene placed both arms about her waist, suddenly drawing her so close that to retain her balance she had to lean back against him. His face was moving against her dark hair, and she felt his lips against her temple.

"You smell sweet, darling. You look beautiful tonight too."

The words were low, almost the first words of love he had spoken to her. Louella was petrified, yet beneath her fear was a surge of emotion she could not define. Naturally she was pleased if he found her desirable. She was too much of a woman to deny this, even to herself. Any woman would feel the same. She grew still, knowing that she should not have come to this place again. Some agent beyond her own resolution had taken from her the will to refuse.

The moon grew brighter, seeking them in this bewitching hour. Eugene's caresses were like a drug, lulling her to acquiescence.

"I don't think you should," she said.

"Tell you how beautiful you are? Why not? Isn't that what a woman always wants her husband to say?"

"You're going too fast . . . " Her voice was unsteady.

"Am I darling? You like the necklace, don't you?"

"Yes, but that doesn't shake my resolution . . . " she faltered to a standstill when his laughter reached her.

"You can't say it. I believe you're beginning to like me."

"I've always liked you — why not? That's nothing to do with this."

"Quite sure? If you'd turn your head slightly this way you'd find my face just near enough for a kiss. I think you should, you know."

His coaxing tone made her smile in spite of herself. "I couldn't."

"But you haven't thanked me for the necklace."

"Thank you. I like it very much. I wish you wouldn't try to persuade me against my inclination."

"You're hard-hearted." He was still

laughing as he turned her slowly towards him. "I won't believe that any woman could be as hard-hearted as that."

She sighed, knowing that she couldn't. His arms were gently compelling as he drew her close and kissed her on the mouth.

"There — you see? Nothing to be scared about over a kiss, is there?" He spoke with brisk kindness. "That was what I was asking for last night, but you had a conscience and ruined everything! Shall we try another?"

Louella thought later that she must have been lulled into acquiescence for she submitted to his gentle caresses. There was no longer any background. Until this moment they had not lived, and she did not make any effort to remember realities. There was insecurity here, a danger of being misunderstood, yet she relied on Eugene, as she could not have done on Clunes . . . "

The name slipped into her mind like a well worn stone into a pool, stirring her to the deeps. She pushed Eugene away, terrified of herself. What had come over her?

"It must be this place — bewitching us both," she said, and she was trembling and cold. "It isn't fair, Eugene. I don't love you. I have to be honest with myself as well as you."

He sighed, and followed her from the summer house. Their moment was gone into oblivion.

They walked back together, not speaking, antagonism between them. When they reached the lawn immediately in front of the hotel she said: "I think we should leave here tomorrow, don't you?"

"Why?"

"Because if we don't I won't vouch for my sanity," she said tartly.

He threw back his head in a roar of laughter, not answering at once. Louella listened to the splashing in the swimming pool as some of the guests took a moonlight swim. It was a delightful sound, utterly refreshing. Eugene had not been fair, or kept to his bargain. He knew all the answers while she did not, and she resented him in some queer, submerged part of her mind.

"Are the others coming?" she demanded vexedly. "They seem to be taking their time. You said the whole unit ... cameramen, technicians, Miss Ashton ... the lot, would be here this week."

"I know, but it was put back for a couple of weeks owing to some hitch. I'd made our plans ..."

"So you just didn't tell me?" she was eyeing him frostily.

"Look here, Louella ..." His brows were beginning to knit with temper.

"I'd like to return tomorrow," she said again.

"All right — we will ... on one condition."

"It isn't right to make conditions."

"It's just this — will you promise to come back here with me one day?"

"How could anyone possibly make such a promise?"

"Will you?" he insisted, his voice rising.

"All right." She was vexed with her

own yielding. One had to be true to oneself, difficult as it was at times. It was no longer any use trying to pretend that she cared for Eugene. Glamour and moonlight had tricked her into almost believing that she did, but she had wakened to reality and the cold wind of sanity.

Eugene followed her indoors. "Listen — they must be dancing in the ballroom tonight. If you insist on going tomorrow at least let's enjoy the few hours we have left."

The insistent beat was stronger, and they could hear the swish of feet on the highly polished floor. Louella went with him reluctantly. She was an excellent dancer, but she had no wish to be drawn into this new atmosphere. Not many couples were dancing, and there was plenty of room. She drew a long breath to steady racing nerves. Eugene smiled and held out his arms. She thought he was probably the best looking man in the room. Oh, dear, it was all such a mix up and she was beginning to lose touch with her old self. Lights were lowered discreetly and for they next five minutes they circled the room together, in an old-fashioned waltz.

"That was — very nice," Eugene said, when the music stopped.

"I prefer something more lively." She spoke perversely, unsure of herself. They danced every dance until midnight, enjoying the hours with a determination that struck her later as being most obstinate. What they found to say to each other she could not remember. Eugene was certainly master of the situation as a younger man could not have been.

At midnight Louella murmured something under her breath.

"I didn't catch that."

She smiled at him in a kindly way. "Like Cinderella I have to go. My glass slipper isn't very durable either."

"Thank you for this evening, darling."

He let her go and she slipped away, wondering if ever a girl had been so mixed up before. He had warned her that he would have a care for his own interests, and she could not blame him for trying.

They returned to the mainland the following day, and were soon aboard ship bound for England.

"Have you enjoyed the trip — on the whole?" Eugene asked her.

"Yes, I have. Thank you for everything, Eugene."

"We can go again in a couple of weeks when the set is on location. Would you like that?"

"I'll think about it."

For the next couple of days slipped back into its former rhythm. She scarcely saw Eugene, although she often heard him about the house. His schedule of work was sometimes so keen that he only emerged from his study for meals. He seldom worked less than four hours a day, and often many more when he was not actually at his desk. Louella came to understand that success had not come without hard work and concentration. She tried to plan her own life around his, making as little change in routine as was possible.

Camille, her nurse, and Sara, had accepted her presence without trouble, and she tried to help them, always reminding herself that she was here probably on a temporary basis. When Eugene realised that she still loved Clunes she did not know what would happen.

Sometimes depression swept her to the point of desperation as she realised that she was no nearer solving her brother's disappearance. If only that could come right she would not have had this sense of failure. All that she had risked had not brought him back into her life. She worried about him constantly, thinking over the circumstances of his flight, trying to find some loophole that had been neglected, but there was nothing. She had gone over it so often that there could be nothing new. She planned fresh ways of advertising, and consulted Claribel on the telephone at least once a day. She felt as if a net were being drawn about her, so tightly that she could no longer see her way clearly.

One evening she felt to have reached the end of her patience.

If only there had been someone in whom she could have confided all her doubts and fears. She sat musing unhappily in her room, until the nurse knocked on her door in passing.

"Someone asking for you downstairs," she said. "Sara wondered if you had retired for the night."

"Not . . . not. . . . ?"

The nurse was on Louella's side and understood the question. "It's not the young man who called last week. This one is quite young. He didn't give any name; just asked Sara for you."

"Thank you, Nurse. How kind of you to let me know."

"I was coming upstairs anyway. Sara told me to let you know." Nurse gave her a smile of encouragement. You never knew with the young ones.

Louella schooled herself to outer calmness before hurrying from the room.

Who could it be? She was relieved that it was not Clunes. If it were her brother then she would have need of all her ingenuity. She felt thankful that Eugene was not in the house.

The young man was waiting in the hall, glancing about him curiously. Sara had not asked him to sit down evidently. He looked up when he heard Louella's step. Suddenly she could not see him for the tears in her eyes. He was here at last.

"Wain . . . oh, Wain . . ."

He strode forward to greet her. "Louella." They shook hands before she drew him into the privacy of the office. When she closed the door she held out her arms and embraced him urgently. They kissed each other before she linked her arm in his.

"You're still my favourite brother. I'm so happy to see you that I don't know what to say." For a moment they were both silent, as she wiped her eyes. "How did you find me here?"

"I went straight to Claribel's flat. That

was the address you left at the news office. I'd seen your enquiry and thought you really must be worried about me. What an odd thing to do — to put an enquiry into the personal column."

"What an odd thing to do — to disappear into the blue — the way you did," she suggested. "Naturally I've been worried. We all have. Oh, I'm glad you are here. Tell me — are you hungry?"

"Ravenous. I hadn't much money with me and decided to sub on you for a couple of days. Finding you was the problem — then Claribel was so keen on getting me here that she never asked me to eat."

"I'll get you something," she told him. "We can talk later. Wait here. Don't move out of this room, will you?" she added anxiously.

She went to the inner door, making sure this time that no one lurked within the ante room, as Eugene had done earlier. She smiled as she went out of the room. The kitchens were in darkness, for which she was relieved.

Evidently Sara had finished for the day. Going to the refrigerator she drew out some cold ham which she made into sandwiches. She added a large slice of apple pie and poured out a glass of milk. She set these on a tray and carried them to Wain.

"These are just what I could find," she set the tray on her desk. "If you are hungry you won't object to the thickness of the bread. I put lots of butter on." She watched as he picked up the plate. His smile of thanks was young, disarming, uncertain. She saw the thin, silky stubble of an embryo beard on his chin. He still only needed to shave about once a week.

"Thanks a lot, Louella. This tastes good." He ate rapidly, and she saw that he was both tired and hungry. Her heart ached as she tried to reason her way through the feelings that swamped her mind. She saw him finish the pie and knew that he was better able to cope with what must be. "I was needing that. It feels good to be full again. I didn't eat all day.

Shall I get rid of the empties for you?"

"No, I'll slip back to the kitchen with them and then we must talk." She placed the used dishes in the sink, before hurrying back to her brother. "I think we'd better go up to my room to talk. I'd hate us to be interrupted, and it's probable that Eugene will be back in an hour or less."

It was about ten o'clock as Louella led him up to her room. His eyes, so like her own, roved about with curiosity in their depths. He stood for a minute, the handle of the door retained in his hand.

"My — this is luxury. Very different from what's been happening to me. So this is what's happened to *you* since you left home?"

She motioned him to a big, velvet covered chair. "You'll be comfortable there, dear. We can talk here without interruption. I want to know every single thing about you and what you have been doing."

She sat facing him, anxious to see his expression while they discussed past and future. She handed him a packet of cigarettes.

"Smoke, Wain."

"Thanks." He relaxed visibly, his long, thin fingers at ease in his big chair. "You do yourself proud around here. What happened?"

"Didn't Claribel tell you I was married now?"

"Yes, but she was in such a hurry to get me over here that I didn't grasp all the story. Am I to meet your husband?" He blew a cloud of smoke contentedly as he spoke.

"Later perhaps. He's out just now. I want to hear about you, Wain. I've been terribly worried about you."

"Was it mean of me to just clear off?"

"Just a moment — I want you to understand that I believe every word you say. I always have and always shall."

He glanced at her in surprise. "Naturally. When did I ever lie to you? It's not been one of my habits . . . "

She saw they were at cross purposes, and some of the burden of guilt and fear began to loosen its hold. She came to him and knelt on the soft carpet at his feet, her hands crossed earnestly on his knees.

"Wain — the night you left home something terrible happened — did you know about it?"

His hand was arrested, his green gaze came to her anxious face. "What do you mean? Is he — dead? Father, I mean . . . "

She bent her head, hiding her feeling. He didn't know. He genuinely didn't know. Her belief in him rose triumphantly to the surface. She had sometimes suspected that he had not known what happened on the night he ran away from their home. Otherwise he would have returned.

As quickly and simply as possible she told him. "The night you left an old woman was assaulted by someone who stole her money. You remember who I mean — she lived at the corner house?" She named the victim quickly, watching his expression.

"Yes, I know who you mean." He lost his colour slowly. "Did they think — as

I was missing — that I'd assaulted her? Did they, Louella?"

She nodded. "I never thought so."

"Did Father?"

"No, but our stepmother did." Her soft lips hardened at the memory.

"Yes, she would. Louella, until this moment I didn't know she'd been hurt or lost her money."

His earnestness held a genuine ring. "You don't need to say that to me."

"Bad luck I chose that night," he commented out of a short silence. "Someone must have used me to cover up."

"Who?"

He shook his head in a troubled way and they both stayed lost in thought. "Didn't they look any further than me? Did they assume that it must be me?"

"The police were called in of course and have been searching . . . "

"I wasn't hiding. Why didn't they find me? I've been working quite openly on a farm." His tone was incredulous, unbelieving.

"Sometimes the more obvious events

208

are most baffling."

"So you left home too? Well, this is a blow all right, Louella. I'll have to face the music, but surely when the old dear sees me she'll recognise that I'm not the man who stole her cash? Yes, that's it. She'll identify me, even if they've lost all the real clues."

She sat back on her heels, her eyes on his brightening face. "Wain dear — a couple of days before I broke away from home — she died from her injuries."

"Oh, no . . . " he shielded his thin face with his hand.

"I couldn't take an more. The funeral was a big one. Every one seemed to shun us. It was ghastly."

He gasped with pain. "Did father . . . ?"

She drew him to her fiercely. "He never believed it either, oh he didn't, but he was bitterly hurt, dear."

He sighed. "I know. What rotten luck . . . to light out that very night . . . oh, blast . . . what shall I do?"

"Different ones suggested that you had left the country."

"How could I? I'd only about seven pounds, after paying for the canoe." He flushed at the implication. "Oh, they thought I'd have plenty, I guess?"

"Yes. Oh, Wain, I can't tell you how grateful I am to see you and have this out with you, although I believed in you all the time. Now I'm happy, because this can be faced in some way. I've got money, and whatever you decide to do I'll help you — all the way."

"Oh, I've been saving my wages. I must have nearly thirty pounds in the post office now. By the way, what did they do with my canoe?"

"It was in the loft when I came away."

"I could just do with it — it's been in my mind to ask you to send it on," he added. The words more than anything yet, confirmed his innocence in her mind. He told her where he had been living, on a farm far from any town. He had always enjoyed country life and had taken the first employment that offered. He was saving up to go to Canada. "I hoped you might join me there, Louella. I'd planned lots of things to get us out of that hole." He leaned both elbows on his knees as he considered the situation. "You know, I may never get clear of this . . . " he added.

The same thought was in Louella's mind. While they were talking she heard Eugene enter the house. Somewhere a clock struck eleven.

"Keep your voice low," she whispered. "I'll let you out presently. I don't feel that you ought to meet Eugene tonight until we have planned something." She knelt up in sudden fear. "What am I saying? I can't turn you out. Where would you go? The police are looking for you. It's a wonder you reached London safely."

How could she let him go, perhaps to be lost again somewhere in the city. He might lose confidence and choose to disappear rather than face his accusers. Because he had not known he had been untroubled — now that he knew, he was a marked man.

They heard Eugene come up the stairs,

211

pass the door to enter his own room. Wain got to his feet. "He'll be coming in here."

"No — I promise you — he won't."

His gaze met hers anxiously, full of doubt.

"He won't. Don't say any more about that now. You'll have to stay here tonight; I can't think of any other way. We can plan something before morning."

"I'll go back — I know I have to go back," he whispered, "but I'd like the privilege of giving myself up rather than being yanked in by the ear, or something." His light words were intended to relieve the burden of strain between them. Louella could not smile. Somehow she must find a way to help him to return, without first being caught. He might even meet Clunes, which would be a disaster, for Clunes believed him guilty. What a muddle it all was, she thought distractedly.

They stood in the middle of the floor, pondering what to do.

"I'd better tell Eugene . . ." she whispered.

"Need you? Does he know about me?"

"He knows I have a brother, but not what has happened."

"You know, Louella, I don't quite like the set-up. Can't fathom what's really happened to you. You're different — in lots of ways." His brilliant green eyes were accusing.

Louella tried to explain the position. "I needed money quickly, for you. Now I have it and it will all be yours. I like Eugene very much."

"But you liked Clunes and when I think back . . ."

They had always been close friends and had turned to each other for comfort when their mother died.

"Let's not remember," she told him painfully. He was listening to the sounds in the quiet house, his manner reserved, abstracted.

"You could stay here — in this room, I mean."

"Don't be absurd. I'm not spending the night in your room."

"Where else will you be safe? I'll sleep in the spare room, and let you out of here early tomorrow." She felt distracted as she tried to plan a way for them both. "You can't face London tonight, dear."

"What's he like — Eugene, I mean?"

"Kind — but he won't like this."

"Then he won't like it any better in the morning. Tell him now." Wain cut through the indecision suddenly. "He'll not be asleep yet. I'll either stay openly, or go to the police tonight. That might be the better way — otherwise you're harbouring a criminal, my girl."

Louella shook her head sadly, wondering what to do for the best. Obviously Wain must give himself up, or he would be picked up which would be a great deal worse. She longed for the council of someone older, and suddenly she decided to consult Eugene.

"Shall I bring him here?"

Wain lighted another cigarette before answering. "Why not?"

She unlocked the door, turning to smile at him.

"We'll both abide by whatever he advises?"

"Yes. He can't have any axe to grind."

She slipped through the partly open door into the darkened corridor. There was a light showing beneath Eugene's door, and she tapped gently before her courage oozed away. Too late she realised her dishevelled state.

The door opened so quickly that she thought he must have been behind it. She shrank from the look on his face. Coming on top of the turmoil of the past few days, and of the harassing hour through which they had lived, she felt she could not cope with this new crisis.

"What do you think you're doing?" he challenged. He was so changed that she felt heartsick and anxious. What was he thinking?

"I — I wanted to ask you something, but it doesn't matter . . . "

His mouth was set in a grim line. "Thought you'd better be discreet? Do you honestly think that I don't know who you've got in your room? Are you wise, Louella? You can try me too far, you know."

She could not make an immediate answer, but relief struggled uppermost.

"It's not Clunes, if that's what you are thinking. I didn't realise how it must appear to you — to others. It's my brother, Wain. Will you come and meet him, please? We're in dreadful trouble and don't know what to do. I'm — sorry to drag you into it, but there doesn't seem to be any other way." Her trembling voice rang with feeling.

Eugene put one hand to his face as he stood watching her. His silence was a rebuff, and she broke into anxious explanation.

"I — I gave him a meal, then brought him up to my room so that we could talk without interruption. He's twenty, and we don't know what to do. We thought — we hoped you might decide." Her coldness and fear reached him at last.

Slowly he drew her nearer in the darkened hall, the only light that shining behind him, for she had closed her own door. He studied her in silence, while she tried to meet the probing stare of his eyes. It was impossible and she broke away. What he had thought was utterly wrong and separating.

"Yes, I'll come. For a while I thought you had Clunes in there with you and I could have murdered him. I'll not have that kind of thing in this house."

She gave him back look for look, not answering.

He said, "Forgive me. I should have known. Come on." He followed her to her room, where Wain was waiting in the middle of the floor. There was an apprehensive look on his young face. Eugene nodded coldly, when Louella made the necessary introductions. Their relationship was striking, for both had the same green eyes, black hair, creamy skins. Wain would grow into a handsome man, but now he was a boy and a very harassed one at that.

Eugene's manner changed perceptibly. Louella wondered if she had dreamed the previous bitterness. He disarmed Wain, talking casually to cover the initial awkwardness of their meeting.

"I knew Louella had a brother but when you didn't come to the wedding I concluded she had broken with you, as with other members of your family."

Louella knelt on the carpet again, close to her brother. She was subdued and afraid. Eugene's eyes narrowed calculatingly as he saw their growing uneasiness.

"Wain and I haven't met since he left home about three months ago. I advertised for him, he answered, coming here tonight direct from Claribel's flat."

"Thank you. That clears the position a bit. Why did you advertise, may I ask?"

"I left home, because I couldn't bear what was happening. You see, the night Wain left home, an old lady was assaulted and her money stolen . . . She died two days before I came away," Louella whispered.

"Well?" Eugene reserved judgment.

"It wasn't me," Wain spoke for the first time. "I didn't know about it until Louella just told me. I came when I knew she was worried about me but I haven't been hiding — why should I?" He gave Eugene a similar explanation to the one he had given his sister earlier.

"I believe you. What are you planning to do now?"

"We hoped you would advise us. Wain feels that as he must give himself up he would like to do it in his own way."

"I agree. It would be wiser than allowing someone to recognise him."

"Suppose they don't believe me?" Wain muttered. "What clues will there be after all this time? They must have reason to suspect me. The police don't go on hunches — only facts."

"You won't be convicted on circumstantial evidence alone." There was a warmer note in Eugene's voice. "In your shoes I would return voluntarily. Give all the assistance you can, and let them sort it out."

"I wish she hadn't died," Louella said. "She would have known it wasn't Wain."

"Are they dead sure it happened the same night?" Wain swung round on his sister incredulously. "Might have been the previous night. Anytime. This is a murder case, sir . . . "

They both gazed at Eugene in growing horror. Until now that word had not come into the conversation.

"I meant him to stay here tonight," Louella explained. "He couldn't leave tonight, could he? In the morning I could go with him perhaps?"

"Yes. You want to go north, don't you? I've got that right? I don't see why you shouldn't. Well, stay here tonight, and tomorrow I'll run you wherever you wish to go. You can sleep in the spare room."

"Aren't you harbouring a criminal?" Wain asked scathingly.

"If I thought so I wouldn't do it," Eugene said, and he was smiling.

Louella sighed gently, forgiving him much for those words. "I'll get you another snack, dear."

"Bring me something, too," Eugene said. "This sort of thing always makes me hungry."

Both men were glad of the hot strong coffee she made. Later she led Wain to the spare room, and saw that he was comfortable, before leaving him. Eugene awaited her return.

"You'll want to go with him in the morning, I suppose?"

"Yes — please."

"Frankly I can't see why he won't give himself up to the London police; why has he to go home, I mean?"

"He feels a thing about it," she told him. "Good night, and thank you for everything." The coldness was back in her voice.

He studied her. "You're very unhappy, aren't you?"

"Yes." She tried to evade his scrutiny.

"This will pass. One thing — will you give me an honest answer — was it for Wain's sake that you accepted my offer so readily?"

"Yes." The word stood alone, stronger because she could not clothe it with explanations.

"I've often wondered the real cause. I'm glad to know."

"I love him so much," she said. "We're alone now. Wouldn't you have done as much for someone you loved?"

"I think so. You're tired, aren't you. Go to bed and try to sleep. In facing this trouble Wain will win through to happiness for both of you. Will you forgive my bad temper earlier? Can't explain it. I'm not such a brute usually, am I, Louella?"

She turned away, too distressed to answer. After a brief hesitation he left the room, closing the door quietly after him.

Louella could not sleep, and she wakened Wain before seven o'clock. They breakfasted early with Eugene. He had already had his big car serviced, and was preparing for the long drive north.

"It's very kind of you," Louella murmured, trying to have a warmer feeling towards Eugene.

Wain ate a hearty breakfast in spite of his natural anxiety. He smiled across at his brother-in-law, and Louella realised that they liked one another.

"Use my overcoat," Eugene offered when he saw that Wain had no coat with him. "It's a cold morning. I'll have my mac."

They all sat in the broad front seat, Louella between the two men. For a while they talked without effort as the big car swung out of the Embankment. Suddenly, across the road, Louella saw Clunes coming towards them. She drew in her breath sharply.

"Look — it's Clunes."

"He haunts us," Eugene explained, his lips hardening with displeasure.

"Keep going." Wain sank lower in his seat.

"You know Clunes too? Of course you would. Did he recognise you?" Eugene asked.

"I wonder." Louella glanced over her shoulder. "I hope not. If he did then anything can happen."

She bent and kissed Wain gently on the cheek. "Perhaps he didn't see you — let's have faith."

Eugene watched them, and his hand came down on Louella's in brief comfort. She felt a surge of gratitude towards him, knowing that he meant to see them through. She felt that he would get them to their destination. She tried to forget all that was unpleasant between them and to remember only what was good.

4

THEY were all preoccupied and quiet as Eugene drove his car along the Great North Road. Louella realised that Wain was seriously worried, and probably dreading the ordeal ahead of him. Although she was so convinced of his innocence, others were not.

"Do you believe that Wain is innocent?" she asked Eugene.

"I do. I said so last night."

"Clunes said it was just blind faith on my part, but if you believe too . . . " She gave Eugene a small, wistful smile.

"Don't mind me," Wain said energetically. "I'm just the man on trial."

Louella pressed his arm warmly. "You're not — you're a darling. We'll see you through and you must try not to worry." For the first time in her life the words identified her with Eugene, but even without his help she would go on. Now that she had the money she could and would do so much.

"Do you want to stop anywhere for coffee?" Eugene said about noon.

"No, let's go on," Wain sounded impatient. They were making good progress, and he longed to drive the car about which he asked many questions. Louella often glanced over her shoulder. "Remember Lot's wife — and stop making me nervous, honey."

Occasionally they broke into conversation, about serious matters, while Louella listened, handing out sandwiches until they had had enough.

"We should arrive by six o'clock," Eugene said, glancing at his watch. The sun was glinting on the fields on either side of them, for they kept as far away from towns as possible. His determination was impressive and comforting, and Louella began to feel that they would gain their objective. If only Clunes had not recognised them, and alerted the police. He was a public spirited man and might feel it was his duty. She tried to turn her thoughts outward, to make these hours memorable for Wain, who had so much to face.

"When you get through this business what are your plans?" Eugene asked late in the afternoon.

"I'd like to go to Canada. I'm keen on farming. It's all so much more scientific than it used to be, and these last three months have proved that I can hold down a farming job. It's been good experience."

"You always loved the country," Louella spoke in a dreamy voice. "I'll come with you and we'll . . . we'll . . . "

Eugene looked at her. "Remembering your — obligations?" There was nothing unkind in the reminder, but she flushed as if he had rebuked her. For a moment she had indeed forgotten her marriage. Her heart ached as she pondered what would be the outcome.

"I feel sometimes as if Fate had singled us out for special attention. Let's live a day at a time. It's the only way to get through."

Eugene nodded and glanced across her to Wain. "You two are remarkably alike in colouring. No one could possibly mistake you for other than brother and sister."

"We take after our mother who was Italian — but I'm like my father in stature. He's very tall, isn't he, Louella?"

"Yes." She thought about their father for a while, feeling miserable. What was he going to think now?

She leaned back, feeling the weariness and strain of travelling, and presently Wain drew her to lean against his shoulder. "That is if Eugene doesn't want me to drive for a change?" he said.

Eugene's eyes were bloodshot with the strain of keeping the car on the road. "No, thanks. We'd better not risk anything."

"Lean back, Louella." Wain put his arm about her shoulders and she relaxed, her half closed eyes on Eugene's stern profile. Without his help today she wondered how they would have managed. Wain hummed below his breath, a soft melodious jumble of sound that wove a bewitchment over her tired brain and body. Presently she fell asleep, turning her face into his shoulder, her hand in his.

Eugene glanced at them from time to time, seeing their genuine love for one another. There had not yet been time for them to grow apart, to lose the feeling that had come through with them from childhood.

Louella wakened when the car stopped. She sat up, one cheek a brilliant pink, the other pale. She rubbed her eyes confusedly.

"We've arrived," Wain said, shifting his arm. "You must be putting on weight, honey. My arm is just about paralyzed."

"Sorry." She followed him from the car, while Eugene rested against the wheel. He looked tired in spite of his jaunty air. "Aren't you coming in with us?" It was almost six o'clock she realised as she glanced at her wrist watch.

"Do you want me to?" Her gaze met his.

"Yes, please." He strode after them into the police station. Louella thrust her hand under Wain's arm, trembling now that the ordeal was upon them. "God bless you always, dear Wain . . . "

He pressed her hand. He walked forward proudly.

"I'm Wain Ford. Were you looking for me?"

The minutes following those quiet words were utterly confusing. Louella stood on one side, watching her brother and Eugene as they answered the seemingly endless questions. Finally Wain kissed her and was led away. She stared after him, paralysed by the thought of where they must be taking him.

"Oh, God, look after him — please look after him . . . "

"I think He will," Eugene said, taking her arm. "Let us go outside. There isn't anything more that we can do for the moment. I've promised Wain the best help and advice there is to be found in England. I've my own man in London, of course." He was talking to draw her away from the tears that threatened. "Would you like to see your father while we are in the district?"

She stood on the pavement, forlorn and uncertain, tears beginning to pour down her face. "No."

"Don't you think he should be told what has happened? It will be a greater shock to him when he finds out tomorrow. You should go to him if only for a few minutes."

"Do you think so?" She got into the car, not knowing what to do without his prompting.

"I'll drive you there now, perhaps?"

"I couldn't bear it yet. Later perhaps?" She struggled to subdue her tears, anxious not to antagonise him.

"All right. We'll go to an hotel and tidy up . . . have a meal. How about that?" His voice was brisk and kind, although he must be tired.

"Thank you."

He presently drew up before an hotel, one she had not entered before. They entered, and for the first time she considered their plight.

"We haven't any luggage."

"Still time to buy a toothbrush." He was not displeased the way events were shaping. "I'll book in then we can relax."

She stood aside, not caring what happened. The long travel coat she was wearing was creased with long sitting, and she felt hot and dishevelled.

Presently she accompanied Eugene to the lift, where they were taken to the third floor. She was not curious as to the accommodation he had booked. Her mind was engaged with Wain's troubles, only working on one circuit, she told herself wearily.

Their rooms were next to each other. Eugene opened her door with a key, handing it to her. "I'm next door. Can you be ready in half an hour? I'm hungry."

The room was cool, the late sunshine slanting across the open windows. She threw off her hat and coat with a sigh of relief. She stood for minutes looking down into the busy street.

Presently she realised that she was not even thinking. Her mind was blank. The sounds Eugene made next door as his washing water gurgled down the pipes, came to her clearly, reminding her that she must hurry.

She was ready when he knocked on her door.

"I never thought to come back to this town," she told him. "Are we eating in the hotel?"

"Yes, I've ordered a meal." He locked her door and dropped the key into his pocket. His grey suit looked none the worse for wear, she thought. She still felt crumpled but refreshed.

"You've been very kind. I'm grateful," she said as they waited for the lift to ascend.

"I know. I understand — better than you think."

It was comfortable being with him; he seemed more understanding just then than anyone she knew. They went into the restaurant, sat down at the reserved table, and started the meal. They were both tired but soon revived.

"I hope Wain will be given a good meal," she said thoughtfully.

"He'll have enough." Eugene ordered the sweet from the waiter. "How would you like to dance for a while? It's a good orchestra."

The music rose and fell as the door opened and closed. They finished their leisurely meal before proceeding to the ballroom. They stood watching silently as the couples drifted past them.

"Now, Louella . . ." After the strangeness of the day she felt she would never again be surprised. To be here with Eugene, on such a mission, made her heart ache. Wain's plight would be forever her own. Yet she knew that Eugene wished her to have this pleasure to take her mind off the agony of the day. Life was complex and bitter.

"Or am I just young," she whispered feelingly.

"I don't follow that observation." When she tried to explain he added:

"Some of it may be the hopefulness of youth, but not all. You are finding the true values. We all have to go through the mill of experience. This is the island over again, isn't it? Just the two of us dancing together." The words brought sudden pain to them both, for they could not now recapture those magic moments.

The one dance drifted into many more, tiredness dropped away, and only the warmth and sympathy between them was left. If only they could have had tonight without any previous misunderstanding. But that was impossible. One always had bitter memory, keen regrets.

"This is positively the last dance," she said. Memory was loaded with the sweetness of those nights on the island, she thought. What was she to do? She felt frantic with the pull of instinct and emotion.

"Louella — I've something I must say to you . . ."

"Not now," she pleaded. She was too unsure of herself to be able to talk to him tonight. There was a magic link somewhere in the atmosphere for which she could not account. Of course she disliked the reason for so much that had happened, why then should she pretend to like Eugene.

"By the way, why don't you call me Gene — my friends always do?" he said. "I asked you once before, didn't I?"

"Isn't that reserved *for* your friends?"

"Don't you want to be counted among my friends then?"

The words brought sudden tension to them both. Louella was at a loss how to answer, without antagonising him. She had so much for which to thank Eugene. "Yes, I suppose I do. I'd certainly rather be friendly with anyone than at variance."

"That's not exactly what I meant — and well you know it. You are a most evasive little person — did you know? Well, I suppose right now isn't the time to go into that."

She glanced up and met the steely look in his eyes, not finding it easy to answer. They circled the room again, the music muted and romantic. Lights were discreetly lowered, the night made for lovers. Louella tried to keep her face serene, her mind blank, but it was not easy. After a while Eugene said: "I telephoned to your father, asking him to come here in the morning. I thought it would be easier for you to meet here than at the house. Is that all right?"

"Oh, yes. I didn't want to have to go there. Thank you such a lot."

"Happier now? I thought that might be the reason. You know, Louella, if you could be perfectly frank with me in all things we might get on a lot better. I'm a straightforward sort of chap."

"I'd gathered that." They both smiled at her wry tone.

His step quickened for the final bars of music. "He'll be here about ten o'clock. We'll see what he has in mind and then see a solicitor. Now will you try not to worry any more?"

The kindly words set her at ease. "Thank you. I'll certainly try. You've taken a load off my mind. Why are you doing so much for me? I'm really grateful."

"Do you want a straight answer to that?"

She glanced up at him again, and hesitated. "No. I don't think so."

He laughed abruptly. "Do you want a drink before you go up?"

"No, thank you . . . but you do. Oh, I've enjoyed the dancing. I just can't understand how I've managed to enjoy the end of such a day."

"No? I'll see you to your room and have a drink later." They went towards the lift, along the silent corridor to her room, where he opened the door with the key from his pocket. She held out her hand for the key, which he dropped into her palm.

"Good night, Eugene — and thank you again."

"Gene . . . " he prompted, smiling. "Don't you think you could find a prettier way of thanking me than just saying the words?"

"Is there anything better than the spoken word?"

He drew her to him quickly. "Don't try me too far, Louella. You know what I want."

His sudden ruthlessness frightened her, and she tried to evade him. "I wish you wouldn't, Gene. It isn't fair to either of us."

"What's a kiss between friends?" he murmured. He was determined and she gave in for the sake of peace. "We are friends after all."

Her mouth was sweet and Eugene kissed her several times before releasing her. Louella tried not to respond, willed herself into a negative role. When she thought of Almira Ashton in his arms, receiving his kisses, it was not difficult to resist him. She stayed passive until he released her.

"Blast . . ."

"Goodnight — and thank you again," she said, looking up at him.

"You did that deliberately." He was fuming, his eyes holding hers with a strange message in their depths. "What's the matter with you? I could remind you . . . "

"If you do — then it's the end," she said quietly.

The words pulled him up as she hoped they would. She must be more careful in future. He turned away, and she watched him walk back down the long corridor before entering her room. She felt shaken as she leaned against the door. The look he had given her was hard to define. She tried to analyse it but failed. Let him get back to his Almira, she thought. Evidently her kisses are satisfactory.

She went to bed and to sleep as if she never meant to waken. Eugene's peremptory knock the following morning awoke her to the new day with its gathering responsibility.

"I'm coming." She dressed at top speed, for she realised that her father would be with them in less than an hour. Eugene awaited her in the writing-room. "I know I'm late. Thank you for wakening me."

"Good morning, Louella." He was clean shaven, brisk, completely at ease as he lowered the newspaper. "What it is to be young. Would you like some breakfast — I've had mine."

"Coffee — I seldom eat breakfast."

Promptly on time, they heard Mr. Ford asking for them at the desk, and Eugene went to meet him. Louella waited in the writing-room which was deserted. Her father entered, followed by Eugene. The moment she had secretly dreaded was upon her. She waited, hands clenched together, until she saw his face. All rebellion fled, and she rushed across the room, into his arms. He returned her kiss with a tenderness she had forgotten. They laughed as they hugged each other.

"My dear . . . " Mr. Ford held her gently, so overcome that he could not give her the greeting he had prepared.

"Daddy . . . isn't it lovely to be together again?" She led him to a settee, while Eugene watched them, an enigmatic look on his face. He was lounging near the door, not taking any part in the reunion.

"Yes. I'm so thankful to see you again — to know you're safe . . . " Mr. Ford's voice was husky.

"I was wrong, daddy — and when I saw you I realised. Have I hurt you? I didn't mean to . . . "

He cleared the huskiness from his throat again. "The same with me. Thank God it's over. What a surprise all this is, too . . . was *he* the reason why you went to London?" He glanced across at the lounging figure.

"Eugene? No. It's a long story, daddy. One day I'll tell you. Wain's affairs seem more important than mine at the moment. Were you shocked last night when Eugene telephoned the news to you?" She held his hand and smiled warmly into his careworn face. Her father had aged since last she saw him.

"In a way, but it ended the suspense. I'm to see Wain today. I'm glad he gave himself up; it was the only thing to do. Eugene said he hadn't known anyone was searching for him. It's all so strange."

She tried to lift the sadness from him. "He's been working on a farm miles from anywhere, just saving up, not even reading the newspapers. They had a radio but he is certain nothing came over the air about him. No, it's just one of those things. If I hadn't advertised for him and his attention been drawn to it, this might have gone on for months."

Eugene drew nearer, sat on one of the tables, smoking. "It was only when the old lady died that the affair became really serious."

Mr. Ford nodded thoughtfully. There was nothing in the situation that he had not reviewed many times. "He went to you . . ."

"Yes. Shall we get down to basics? We want to do all we can for him."

Mr. Ford looked from one to the other curiously. "You are kind to take to much interest in Wain. Is it because you love Louella?" It was a natural assumption on his part, but Louella shrank from the question. She waited for Eugene to reply.

"Could be. I'll see my own lawyers in London; I'm already in touch with them. We must get the best counsel we can for Wain." They discussed what had happened from every angle, in agreement on all points.

"I'm not a poor man," Mr. Ford pointed out. "I can do what is necessary. You were planning this without me, of course — but I want a share now."

It was almost noon when he left them, and Louella felt happier.

"Would you come home with me for a meal if I asked you?" he said.

Louella softened her refusal with a kiss. "No — I couldn't yet, daddy. Give me time. Perhaps when Wain is with us again."

He sighed, knowing he had not the right to expect so much. "All right, dear. I understand." He turned at the door to wave to them, and was soon out of sight in the busy street.

"You wanted me to stay during the

interview, didn't you?" Eugene said.

"Yes." She walked with him to the dining-room.

"I wanted to see you greet your father."

She looked at him askance. "Why?"

"You are a perpetual surprise to me, Louella. I got your measure wrong in the first place, and have been doing some reorganising since then." The brisk words made them both laugh as they seated themselves at a table. " It's early but we should get something. I want to be on my way immediately after lunch. Or would you prefer to stay on alone?"

"I'd sooner return with you, because I can't see Wain again if I stay." Life in London was more real to her than all the previous years she had spent in the north. "You want me to return, don't you?"

"I think you are wiser to return. You're too attractive to be wandering around on your own."

They left the hotel in Eugene's car. Louella's eyes clouded with tears when they faced the open fell country again.

Life held so much of light and shade, and they were walking in shady places now.

"Could we go via Newby Bridge?" she said when they approached Windermere. "Wain used to love it down there. I'd like to see it again."

"Easy," he agreed casually, and put the car into the steep decline to Bowness. "I believe he told me that he used to do some canoeing there."

"Yes." They stopped at the exact place where they had picnicked two years before. "It's amazing that so much can happen in so short a time. We were happy then." She sat down to muse. "Mother was alive then, I was still at college, father hadn't lost any money or at least not much, Wain came round that bluff — and tea was waiting. It was a happy day."

Eugene stood behind her, allowing her to muse until he reminded her that time was flying, and they had far to go. She sighed, stood up, and shook the grass from her skirt. She doubted if she would ever come here again.

Late in the evening, dusk falling, lights springing up in the towns, they were both quiet, tired with the journey and their thoughts.

Presently Eugene drew into a layby, and the sudden silence as the engine smoothed out, was uncanny. Traffic was increasing, the cars passing monotonously, but in this quiet place they could be alone. He stretched and brought out his cigarette case, offering her a cigarette.

"Tired?" she said, accepting one, with a smile of thanks.

"Yes, we'll halt here for a few minutes." He lighted both cigarettes and they smoked companionably for a while. "I don't enjoy hours of driving as I used to do. Must be getting old."

"Thirty-three isn't old," she remonstrated.

"No? I'm ten years older than Clunes — that's quite a step."

"Oh dear — why bring him into it?"

"I want to talk seriously to you, Louella."

The challenge was between them again and she recoiled. "No. I can't — can't stand it tonight. Please . . . "

"You'll have to face it sooner or later
— why not now?" His quiet determination
baffled her.

"Let it be later then," she said. "Besides,
you promised . . . six months you said."

"Yes." He hesitated. "Well, perhaps not
now, but after I return from Edinburgh I
think we must have a serious talk about
many things."

"When do you go to Edinburgh?"

"Tomorrow. Surely I told you about
it? Would you care to come with me?
That's quite an idea. We're flying . . . "
He turned to her eagerly as if he expected
her to agree.

"No. I don't want to go. Will — Almira
Ashton be going too?" She could not
resist the question.

He was smiling. "Yes. Almira will be
there all right. You know, it will be an
interesting experience. I've been to the
Film Festival before but I don't believe
you have. Why not come along?"

She longed to accept but decided
against doing so. Already she felt that

Eugene was taking too much for granted.

"No. Thank you all the same. I would be out of my element."

"Any excuse is better than none, eh?" His expression was unreadable. "Just as you wish then. When I return we'll have that talk."

"About Wain?" The words came reluctantly. "I suppose you think I should have told you about him before . . . our marriage?"

"It might have been wiser but we'll not quarrel on that score. No, it's not that particularly that we must discuss. You've too much on your mind just now so we'll leave it for the time being." He threw the cigarette through the open window and stretched again as if tired. "Ready? We'll soon be home now. You must be tired after the double trip. It's the monotony that's pretty deadly, isn't it?"

His smile was charming, but she felt baffled by the reserve in his manner. Was he annoyed with her, in spite of his reassurance? Life had certainly not been even since they had met. First Clunes, then Wain. She drew her coat about her, hugging herself, trying to look warmer than she felt. The rug had slipped down and he tucked it about her.

"Thank you. It's the cold, snaky feeling when one's fuel is running out," she spoke faintly. "Eugene — am I being unkind?"

He played with the gears for a moment before answering. "If you are it's with good intention. Shall we leave it at that?"

She nodded miserably. She turned from him in distress.

He said: "I wonder how Wain is feeling right now?"

Louella wondered, too. For the remainder of the journey they were silent. When they entered the house an hour later Louella thanked him before leaving him. Camille was hovering on the stairs, and she hurried up to the child, glad of any distraction. They hugged each other and the child was reassured.

"You wented without telling me," Camille complained sweetly.

"You weren't up . . . "

"We thought you'd gone to Russia, Louella?"

"Why Russia?" Louella enquired wonderingly.

"'Cos you were so long." The explanation was made scornfully. "Are you cold?"

Louella shivered realistically. "Yes — just as cold as if we really had been to Russia. I'm longing for a hot drink. Come to my room, darling, while I change." She took the child by the hand, and Camille played happily while she washed and changed. Presently they drank the hot coffee that was sent up by Sara. Louella carefully added milk to Camille's cup. "You're getting quite grown up, darling. Now it really is long past your bedtime." Louella swept the child up into her arms and carried her up to the nursery. "Not a muff out of you remember or we won't be allowed a late night rendezvous again . . . "

Camille was sleepy, and she clung to Louella until she was safely in bed. The child was evidently relieved to know that they were safely back.

"All this coming and going can't really be good for her," Louella said later to Eugene after they had dined. "She must wonder what it's all about. This time I'm the guilty cause, but I've tried to make it up to her. I'm grateful for all you have done — and intend to do," she added nervously.

They were seated near the fire in the lounge, for there was a storm rising outside, and rain was already lashing against the windows. Eugene was leaning back in his armchair, apparently lost in thought. The evening paper was across his knees. Louella crouched on a stool staring into the fire, which shone on her dark hair.

Eugene's half closed eyes missed nothing during that hour together. Presently he said, out of a long silence: "Louella, promise me you won't decide anything about Clunes until I get back from Edinburgh."

She raised her head restlessly, not answering.

"We've not given ourselves a chance yet to discuss everything. Until we can agree I think you should keep him away from here. It shouldn't be difficult — you seem able to cold shoulder a man most successfully."

"I resent that."

"I beg your pardon. It wasn't intended to be anything but a bit facetious. I'm not in a joking mood, Louella."

She turned to him generously. "I won't see him if I can avoid it. He said he wouldn't come until midweek — so you'll be back."

"He was on his way here the morning we set off with Wain," he spoke dryly as if she were overlooking this point.

"Only yesterday morning," she marvelled. " What a lot has happened in forty-eight hours. I certainly won't make matters any worse than they are if I can help it."

"Just so long as we understand each other." His hard expression did not change and she wondered what were his thoughts. "I don't want gratitude from you, Louella. That's a cold feeling."

"No. It's warm and vital. No matter how old I grow I'll never forget what you have done for Wain." She tried to make him understand but felt how inadequate were her words.

"You both have a knack of putting yourselves in the wrong — but you are sound underneath."

The casual words comforted her. She rose to her feet swiftly. "Thanks, Eugene. I'm going now. Goodnight."

"Just a moment." He put the paper aside and followed her.

She stood with her back to him. "Please let me go. I can't stand any more tonight."

"All right. I have your promise," he reminded her.

She sped from the room, thankful to make her escape. She knew that on his return from Edinburgh the issues at stake must be faced. Uneasiness regarding her position added to the burden of anxiety over Wain. She sat down to write to him, but abandoned the effort, unable to concentrate. She lay thinking about

Almira Ashton, far into the night, trying to see the way clear for her own future actions.

Eugene left the house the following morning, and for a few days Louella knew she could relax. She spent the afternoon pleasantly, playing in the garden at the back of the house with Camille. Later she went shopping in Kensington, enjoying the power that money brought.

She walked home, taking her time, pondering on so many matters. Her thoughts were happier, and she began to see some order in the chaos surrounding her. She was within shouting distance of the house when Clunes' voice arrested her.

"Louella . . . I've been waiting for you. They told me you were out."

She had been unaware that he was in the vicinity, and the shock of his appearance drove the colour from her cheeks. "You — you promised not to come until Wednesday."

He took her arm deliberately. "I know. You're looking very lovely and I can't stay away from you. There is nothing to do but think and it's driving me crazy. I want to talk to you. Come and have a meal with me."

"I — I can't." She tried to resist him unsuccessfully.

"Your old man's out of town — I learned that from the maid. She thinks I'm a friend of the family." Clunes walked her past the house determinedly. "Come on, Louella — have a heart. We've got to talk."

"Where are you taking me?"

"I'm not going to kidnap you, so come on." His tone was grim.

She held back the angry retort, determined not to lose patience. In this mood he was impossible. "I just don't want to go, that's all. This masterful business won't get you far with me — it never did if you remember. Please be reasonable."

"What's a chap to do? Talk to you I will if I have to walk the streets until dawn."

She realised his determination and

capitulated. "All right." As they walked towards a taxi rank she mentally compared Clunes with Eugene. Eugene's outlook was more sophisticated, adult, seldom allowing him to appear in the wrong. Clunes was younger, more hot headed, bent on obtaining what he wanted. Her expression softened to tenderness as she realised that with all his faults Clunes was the man she loved. She must be careful or this would give him an unfair advantage. Eugene had not the power over her that Clunes had, and this must be the reason.

"I'll have one hour with you — only," she said, smiling at him.

"That's better, darling. All this business is enough to make me head for the river. Get in . . . " He gave an address to the driver, and followed her, banging the door. "Gosh, Louella . . . "

He leaned far back, drawing her with him, and during the short journey she had to submit to his arms about her. They alighted at an hotel, and after paying the driver he followed her indoors.

Louella shivered in the waning sunshine, wondering what the next hour would do to her future.

"I'm hungry. I haven't eaten all day," Clunes said.

"I'm not dressed for a place like this," she demurred.

"You look all right to me."

"Why did you choose to stay at such an expensive hotel?" she asked.

"One must have a good address — even if it's only for a couple of weeks. Nothing succeeds like success. Haven't you heard that before?"

She followed him to a table where they were to dine. Her silk suit was unobtrusively smart and she did not feel as out of place as she had anticipated. She was glad now that she had changed for the shopping expedition earlier.

Clunes ordered, while a waiter hovered respectfully. When he had gone she said: "So much respect; he must think you are a millionaire."

"Stacks of professional people trade on their reputations. It does no harm to make 'em think you're made of money. I will be too one day. You'll see, my sweet Louella."

With her he could not put on airs for they had known each other since childhood. There were no secrets. In his youth Clunes had been wild but he was settling down now, ambitious for a career.

She watched him, her eyes revealing nothing of her thoughts. When the meal was served they satisfied their youthful hunger before speaking on serious topics.

"Now." Clunes pushed his dessert plate aside.

"Well?" Her green eyes hid the sudden apprehension she felt at the change of tone. This was it.

"Did I dream that I saw you with your brother a couple of days ago?"

"No. You did see him."

"Well — aren't you going to tell me what happened. Or is that yet another secret," He leaned forward earnestly.

"Not a secret, and I can tell *you*, of course. Wain came when he knew I was searching for him. Claribel sent him along the evening before you saw him. We took him home so that he could give himself up to the police. That's just about the size of it."

He glanced at her sharply. "There's more to it, surely?"

"Yes — I told him everything, and he just didn't know. When he knew what had happened it changed everything — naturally. He wants it clearing up. You were wrong all the time, Clunes. Wain is innocent."

"It will take some proving after all these weeks," he said thoughtfully. "What did he say when you explained it happened the night he left home?"

"He was upset. It was bad luck that his going coincided with the robbery."

"So he's innocent," Clunes said, gazing across the room.

"You wouldn't believe — do you now?"

"If you say so. Is Eugene defending him?"

"He's getting legal help — yes."

"So where does that take us?" His dark

eyes bored into her suddenly. "He'll not do all that for nothing. You can't kid yourself much longer."

"That's unfair . . ."

"You told me you weren't his wife. Be advised by me before it's too late. Come away with me — tonight. Tomorrow then? I'm on the rack the whole time. It's driving me crazy — wanting you for keeps and knowing you're living near that fellow."

"He's quite nice," she strove to reassure him. "We understand one another. I can't do what you ask. I promised him not to see you — yet here we are . . ."

"When's he due back?" he asked sulkily.

"Tomorrow evening. He's up in Edinburgh . . ."

"With the luscious Almira? Oh, can't you see the set-up for yourself? They're using you; even they couldn't get away without some cover. She's got a husband — he's got a wife — all respectable on the surface."

Louella was silent. Almira had said the same thing, yet she had tried not to listen, to be fair in her thinking. Surely it must be apparent to all who knew Eugene? They must pity her immaturity. Yet she had got something out of the situation — Wain's future. So much Eugene had promised her.

"I can't do anything hastily. He asked me not to. We are going into the whole situation thoroughly on his return. I was too tired yesterday or we'd have sorted it out then."

"I'll bet you would," he sneered. "Can't you see where it will end? You're not so blazing innocent as all that, Louella."

"I resent that. You mustn't speak to me in this way."

"Well, if you can stand that fellow around when you are in love with me . . ." The hard words went into complete silence.

Louella's green eyes flashed with temper. "All right," she said presently. "You win. What do you want me to do?"

Clunes put his hand across the table. It

was a large hand, capable, strong, warm as he grasped hers. "Good girl. Come away with me — tonight . . . "

"I couldn't tonight. It would be too cruel not to let them know at the house. Besides it would precipitate a crisis and a lot of mud would be stirred up. No, think of something better than that."

He pressed her hand. "Just so long as you are willing to come . . . How about explaining things tonight, make your arrangements, leave a note for him. He'll not worry too much. It's a showdown. You can pack your things and get away tomorrow . . . before he returns . . . "

Louella considered. There were so many more sides to the questions than he could know. Camille was one — already they cared for each other and the child would grieve. Then Wain — would Eugene consider his duty complete without carrying out his promise regarding Wain? Thoughts crowded each other as she wondered what to do.

"I ought to see Eugene first. I can't just walk out . . . "

"You can if you love me enough," he said bitterly.

She patted his hand absently, not replying. Suddenly his voice reached her, low, tense, broken.

"Stay with me tonight, Louella. There's more in life than financial gain. Prove to me that you love me, that it's only me you love."

Tears entered her eyes for his pleading was much harder to resist than the previous demanding had been. "I — can't . . ."

"Then you don't love me."

"I do. Don't be so hard, Clunes. Why has it to be now — I don't want to make a mistake for any of our sakes."

"You wouldn't consider anything but me if you loved me."

"You are unreasonable. I love you but there are others to consider. We wouldn't be happy long if we took the quick way out of our troubles. I *am* married — that's quite different from being single . . ."

"What's it amount to? You told me

you hadn't slept together." The jealousy behind the words frightened her. So that was it . . .

"I won't stay if you mean to talk this way." He pulled her back to her chair with one violent movement.

"Well — have you?"

"No."

"All right. So you want to see him first?"

"I'd better. He — he doesn't believe in divorce. He told me so."

Clunes' eyes seemed to burn in their sockets. "So that's it? He won't give you your freedom? Louella, my dear, you've got us into a fine mess, haven't you?"

5

IT was after ten o'clock before Clunes would allow Louella to leave him.

"I didn't want to tell you this," he said finally, "but you take some convincing. I think you hold a torch for Eugene although you won't believe it. I happen to know that this trip of his to Edinburgh isn't as innocent as it appears to be on the surface. Eugene and the lovely Almira are living together . . . and that isn't hearsay . . . "

"You must be wrong, Clunes."

"I'm not. They've lived together for the past two years. Almira told me so herself. I saw her the day after you married, Eugene. Now are you convinced? I can prove it to you too."

She recoiled from the suggestion; she could not bear having this proved by anyone. She accepted his words in despair.

"If you've any sense you'll plan without him."

All the things that Eugene had told her did not stand up beneath Clunes' definite accusation. She wanted to believe him wrong but at that moment she felt he must be right. "Oh, it's ghastly . . . "

"Only because you can't make up your mind, my girl. Once you cut him out you'll feel happier."

"All right." She capitulated suddenly. The crisis was upon her and she must make a choice. "Take me back, Clunes."

Claribel called her on the telephone soon after she returned to the house. "I called three times but you were out."

Louella was depressed. "I was. I know it's late, but could you come round to see me? Stay the night perhaps? Do come if you can."

Claribel agreed blithely. "I'll pack a trunk and be with you in five minutes, darling. Don't sound so gloomy. I've news for you — but it can wait. Bye for now." She rang off, not giving Louella chance to enquire further.

She asked for a light meal to be placed in the study, and she was waiting there when Claribel arrived, complete with nightdress and tooth brush in a cream holdall.

"Darling. Oh, it's nice to see you. I began to think you didn't want to know little old Claribel any more." She placed some papers squarely on the table. "You've been having adventures?"

Louella smiled warmly. "As if that could ever be — no, I've been busy — and worried too since seeing you last." She told her friend what had transpired since she sent Wain to them. "Eugene and I took him back north . . . he gave himself up to the police . . . "

Claribel whistled expressively, and hastened to cover the sound with a short cough. "My mother always warned me that a whistling girl and a crowing hen . . . sorry, you're worried sick and I don't mean to be facetious. Tell all."

Louella picked up the evening papers and dropped them again nervously. "Yes, I'm worried all right — not only about

Wain either. Clunes is back on the front page, and he insists that I leave Eugene and go away with him. He's so jealous that — just anything could happen."

"Oh, no." Claribel was shocked. "What are you going to do?"

"What would you do?"

"That's what's known as a moot point. Never having been in such an uncomfortable position. I wouldn't know. On the face of it you can't go back on your promise to Eugene so soon surely? You must have known that something like this might arise." She looked so stricken that Louella came to her senses abruptly. If her best friend felt so, then it could not be right to leave Eugene. "Why did you go to all this trouble if you meant to quit?"

Louella sank into a chair. "Strange as it seems I didn't go too closely into Clunes' viewpoint. Men are different I guess. I was so angry with him — perhaps that was why."

"Now you aren't? What's he say about Wain now?" Claribel was frankly curious, and eager for information.

"Well, he has to wait and see, hasn't he, but I thought he was much nicer about it than previously."

"So now he means to prise you away from Eugene?" She glanced at the waiting tray mechanically.

"Yes, let's have some food," Louella said. "I've dragged you out after eleven o'clock, and you must be famished. I'm glad you can stay overnight, Claribel. It's always such a relief to have you around." She poured a cup of coffee and handed it to her friend. "What was your news? You hinted you had some."

Claribel accepted a couple of chicken sandwiches and began to eat. "Yes — wonderful news, for me. I'm off to America in ten days' time. Flying. All expenses paid. Marvellous."

"How did all this happen?" Louella didn't look as happy as she should have done. "Of course it is wonderful for you — but what about the rest of your friends — me?" She dreaded the coming parting for Claribel was the one safe island in her rough sea.

Claribel's eyes were thoughtful. "Has it ever occurred to you that you are a bit selfish?"

"It has — I am — but aren't we all? If wanting to hold on to you is selfish then I am." Louella rose to the attack.

"Yes. I suppose we all feel that way at times. I'm going to America for an Agency, who pay all expenses. If I like it out there I may stay. At the moment the plan is only for two months — want to join me? It might help to stave off a decision for a while."

"Don't I wish I could. Oh, yes, if only I could. but it's impossible."

Claribel sighed and reached for another sandwich. "You know best. I suppose you have to stand by. By the way, seen the evening papers?"

"These?" Louella lifted one up again, and opened it.

"Back page — picture — Almira Ashton and . . ."

"Eugene?" Louella turned the pages swiftly until she found what she sought.

The photographer had been skilful, catching the handsome couple as they were about to enter a building. Surrounded by a crowd Eugene was trying to protect the lovely Almira, one arm protectingly about her shoulders. They were both laughing, and on the woman's face was a tenderness and beauty that there could be no doubting.

Claribel watched Louella closely. "Of course the next minute she might have been swearing — who's to know?"

"She's in love with him . . . " Louella's soft mouth hardened.

"You knew that — before." Claribel pointed out. "What you have to find out — is he in love with her?"

"You once said he was . . . "

"Hearsay . . . rash statement on my part. I never met him. You should know him by this time."

"I don't," Louella confessed wearily. If Eugene loved Almira it might solve part of the problem. What was the use of trying to hang on to a marriage that was merely a pretence? Almira had been frank about it at the beginning. Was it on her advice that Eugene had married Louella? The thought burned in her mind uneasily.

"No wonder Clunes thinks he has a good case when he sees pictures like these in the evening papers," Claribel commented.

Louella did not trouble to glance further. She had seen enough.

"You've got to stand by, my love," Claribel murmured. "Don't do anything rash at this stage. How was Wain when you left him? These things pass if we can hang on. You're just going through your bad patch. When it's all over you'll have twenty years of cabbage patch existence. Think how nice that will be?"

"From here it looks a wonderful prospect," Louella admitted. "I wonder what will happen next."

"You really want to know?"

"Why, yes — what do you mean?" Louella was startled by the abrupt question.

"From all you have told me, I

feel that Clunes has guessed right. I deduce too that your husband will start making claims. Aren't you expecting that yourself?"

"No. He isn't like that. We understand each other."

"That's nice — very nice," Claribel conceded.

They glanced at each other uncertainly. "You don't agree? You share Clunes' feeling. Oh, what am I to do?"

"You tell *me*," Claribel begged. "I could remind you — but I won't." She stared into her empty cup with hostility. "You love Clunes . . . "

"I suppose I do."

"There's no supposing about love. You'd better be sure. I've a feeling you didn't — that's why marrying Eugene was so easy."

"Oh? Let's not worry about me any more, Claribel. I'll be all right. Let's talk about your trip instead. Are you taking lots of new clothes?" They discussed Claribel's wardrobe animatedly for a while.

"I'm making several summer dresses. I wish I'd just one couture gown though — just to make an impression on the natives."

"Why not? Claribel, you can have my gold lamé gown — the one I wore at the reception. I never want to see it again. It would fit you."

"Wouldn't Eugene mind? He paid for it, you said so."

"He'll not care; it served its purpose. He wanted me to be the best dressed woman there that evening. I'll get it and you can take it with you in the morning."

"I'll come up with you then," Claribel was sorry for the pain she read in Louella's face. "It's midnight and I need my beauty sleep." She followed Louella into her bedroom.

"Here's the dress — and the original packing — take the lot."

"Gorgeous." Claribel held the shimmering gown in front of her. "If it does for me what it did for you . . ."

"What *do* you mean? I was never so

275

miserable in my life as that night."

Claribel coughed. "I wouldn't know. Just talking through my hat again and that's something I loathe in others. Well, goodnight, honey. Try to sleep. If I think of a solution I'll let you know. Why don't you emigrate to a coral isle or something?"

"Sounds wonderful. I wish I could."

"Yes, I should think you'd adore it — for at least an hour." Claribel went off to the guest room, laughing. Her face was thoughtful however as she prepared for bed. How could Louella withstand Eugene when he had so much to offer that would make her life complete?

Louella was in the breakfast room when Claribel appeared the following morning. Her face was pale and she looked distrait.

"I know — you didn't sleep." Claribel tried to look cheerful as she took her place at the table. "I always seem to be eating when I come here."

"Eugene is coming home tonight — about seven," Louella said. "He just rang to say so."

"Considerate of him."

"It's earlier than I'd expected. Claribel — offer me some advice — even if I can't take it. What am I to do?"

"Don't sound so frantic. What's in your mind? Tell Claribel."

"I don't want to leave with Clunes in an underhand manner — but I can't bear to stay either, although if Almira and Eugene . . . " She glanced down at her plate. "Oh, can't you see? If they are, then your idea that Eugene will — want me . . . must be all wrong. He won't want me, if he has her, will he? Yet both you and Clunes are so sure."

"And he's a man and should know," Claribel was always logical. "You'll just have to take a step at a time — totter along for a while."

"I'm not going to be spineless. He must give up Almira . . . "

They measured glances. "You'd

consider it — then?"

"No. What am I saying? I must be going mad."

"You'd better be sure before you meet Clunes again. Girls have been murdered for less." Claribel spoke dryly. "Look, I have to go — business calls. Sorry — give me a ring if you need me, day or night . . . before the tenth. After that I'll be in America."

Louella sat on long after she had gone. What to do? She roused herself to go up to the nursery.

"I can't go out with you this morning, darling," she told Camille. "Nurse will take you instead. Buy her some ice cream, please, nurse. Have something yourself. Don't forget your mac — it could rain."

The promised treat soothed Camille's disappointment as she departed for her daily outing with the nurse. Louella waved to them from the window, until she heard the telephone ringing downstairs.

"Yes? Who is it? Clunes?" Her hand trembled suddenly. "No, I haven't started packing yet, but I'm going to. Claribel has been here. Why don't you go round to see her?"

"Look, darling, you're going to fulfill our plans, aren't you?" His deep voice held a warning note.

"Yes, I'm starting to pack," she spoke faintly, knowing the decision was made at last.

"I'll call for you about five o'clock. That gives you plenty of time."

"Yes." She turned away from the telephone, distraught. So much to do and so little time to do it. "I can't leave this way . . . yet I must . . ."

She returned to her room and set about packing her possessions. What she was doing seemed more terrible in the light of Eugene's kindness to her. Yet how far had he been swayed by his own wishes in the matter? She wished she could be certain on that point. Both Claribel and Clunes had far more experience in worldly matters . . . she had certainly no intention of playing second fiddle to Almira Ashton. If Eugene expected that then he underrated her.

"I've been mad to agree to go along with him," she thought wearily. "No wonder we've landed in serious trouble." She began to think about Wain again, reviewing every aspect of his case.

The day passed slowly. At four o'clock she wrote a note to Eugene and left it propped up where he could not fail to see it. She walked down the stairs for the last time, to await Clunes.

"Ready, darling?" She answered his ring when she heard the taxi stop in front of the house. Sara was out shopping and the house quiet.

"Yes. It seems a terrible thing to do . . . " Her agitation grew as she saw his determination.

"It's better than sitting around waiting. You'll be all right when we're on our way." He would not give her time to change her mind. "Get in the taxi, darling. We're driving to an hotel near Epping Forest. We can stay there for the time being. I don't want to be too far away for a while as I have another broadcast in a couple of days."

She agreed weakly, and they drove away from the house. It was a relief to leave the bustling traffic of the West End, and merge into lowlier districts. Louella felt withdrawn, pensive, no longer master of her own future. What would Eugene do when he found her gone? After promising that she would not do anything decisive while he was away? Yet he lived his own life, uncaring that she might be hurt.

"Have you got a headache, darling?" Clunes spoke gently, his hand on hers. He seemed more grave today, as if this step they were taking was a responsibility. Was he alarmed now that they were together — that she had agreed?

"Yes. I have." She made it the excuse to stay quietly in her corner as her uneasiness mounted to nightmare proportions. She felt chilled and weak, with Clunes a shadow beside her, no longer a man of substance. A shadow upon her future . . . She gazed at him steadily.

"Clunes . . . I want to go back. Please

take me back. I can't go on. This isn't fair to any of us. There must be another way."

"There's no turning back now," he said soberly. "You're mine. You always have been and now we both know it. Don't weaken, it'll be all right."

"It can't ever be all right," she whispered tragically. "Oh, let me go back. Don't my feelings count?"

"Yes, but not to the extent of letting you go. You'll settle down." The hard words sealed her doom, and she drew back into the corner overcome with dread.

They reached their hotel soon after six, and she followed Clunes indoors. All the arrangements had been made by telephone that morning and there were no embarrassing moments. They were shown up to their room at once, along the quiet, cool corridors.

Louella looked about her, feeling trapped and so acutely unhappy that she could have sat on the stairs and wept. Clunes gave the pageboy a handsome tip when he put their cases down inside the door.

"Now." The door closed and they were alone. "Come here . . . " He held out his arms to her, and she went to him, her feet dragging. His arms closed about her gently at first, more insistently when he felt her lack of response. "What's the matter with you? You love me, don't you?"

She turned her face aside from his eagerness, while panic mounted. This had got to be right, for everything had been contributing to this moment when they would be together. There was no responding glow to his kisses. Something had gone from their relationship and she was frightened. Fear made her rigid. She tried to push him away.

"Let me go, Clunes. Let me go. I — I have to unpack." She was trembling, almost crying in her despair.

"Well — what do you know? You're not the girl I remember. You're cold and selfish . . . or are you leading me on? Is that it? You won't need to try very hard.

I'm mad about you, Louella — I always have been. You know that. You needn't be scared of me. You can twist me round your fingers if you care to — if you care enough . . . "

It was true. She remembered how vulnerable he always was before those he loved. Even now she might get her own way if she could placate him sufficiently.

"I'm not scared of *you* . . . " she said. "It's the situation — everything. It all feels wrong. I wanted it to be different. You remember — the little white church against the fells . . . we meant to be married there. You wanted it too. You said . . . " she was breathing quickly, trying to overcome her nausea of fear and doubt. What was the matter with her? Was she still not sure?

"What's it really matter?" he spoke more gently, moving his head against her shining, dark hair. "It's just the two of us. We haven't lived until now. I'm your man — and it's for always."

"No one — can ever be sure that it's

for always . . . " she whispered. "Oh, Clunes, we seem to have taken all the wrong turnings since I left home. Do you remember . . . "

"Come now, girl, don't start remembering. It's going to be all right." There was a warning behind the quiet words. Was he right? Were her fears just the nervous dread of the unknown? Was she allowing nerves to destroy their happiness in each other? She had allowed herself to be persuaded and surely it would come right in time. She tried earnestly to convince herself as well as Clunes.

"Nerves, Clunes. That's all it can be."

He allowed her to move out of his embrace, but there was a dissatisfaction about him that troubled her. She moved to the window, staring out into the waning light. The hotel was close to the forest, in a splendid position, not far from the main road. She glanced over her shoulder at the room, seeing their suitcases, the big double bed. Clunes was already making the room his own as he opened his case and scattered the contents boldly.

Too late . . . the words seemed to vibrate in the warm air. She turned with a laugh to meet him as he came towards her again. "Clunes — I wish you would lose yourself for a quarter of an hour, until I can get washed and changed for dinner. Please . . . "

"Why shouldn't I stay?" He was grinning mischievously, his good humour restored. "You aren't planning to run away, are you?"

"I shall not leave this room," she promised, and she went back into his arms on the promise.

"All right. I'll go down and have a drink. We'll dine together in half an hour. That all right? See what an accommodating husband I'm going to be." He hummed to himself as he went to the door. He slipped the key from the inner to the outer side of the door. "Just in case you change your mind, darling." His laughing eyes held a warning and she knew that he did not trust her promise to remain in the room. With the key in his pocket he could afford to be generous. Had he guessed her purpose, or part of it? She stood watching him, listening for his firm tread along the corridor outside.

Oh, God . . . what must she do? So little time to do anything. She had noticed the telephone subconsciously, and she went to the instrument without hesitation and picked up the receiver. She scarcely breathed as she gave Eugene's number. There was a chance that he might have already reached the house. If he had not then it was fate — she must think of some other way. She knew that she would never be able to leave Clunes without help. He had her measure and would watch her constantly. For the first time she realised that they were no longer even friends. Clunes wanted her because he had always wanted her, in the same way, yet he was not the man she had once thought she loved.

"I don't love Clunes . . . " she whispered the words in fear. "That's why I'm afraid of him. That's why I left home, because I didn't love Clunes any more . . . not any of those other reasons . . . just that I didn't love Clunes any more . . . " She put her hand over the mouthpiece so that she could not be overheard. The revelation astounded her for she had always accepted that she loved Clunes, even when most angry with him. She tried to concentrate on the constant buzz at the other end of the line. The telephone would be ringing in Eugene's office. Sara would come to answer it if he were not there. She prayed aloud as she waited, stiff with concentration and fear.

"I don't love Clunes . . . " If only she might get a message to Eugene before it was too late. Eugene . . . Her heart lurched as if the room had moved. It was Eugene whom she loved, and now he would never understand. She had put herself forever in the wrong, shown herself ungrateful, undignified. She stood rigidly, a tide of intense feeling rushing over her as she realised — the bitterness of her plight.

How long had the feeling been there unrecognised? She was overcome by realisation. Had she fallen in love with him that first evening in Visby? Was it then that her feeling had changed? Was it because of the misunderstanding about Almira Ashton that she had been unable to accept his word, and distinguish real from false?

The answers could not matter now for she was forever in the wrong. In coming away with Clunes she had thrown away all chance of happiness with Eugene. His patience had been long, but no man could overlook such an action. She was frantic with pain when she realised everything.

"Oh, dear God, help me," she whispered, trembling as she held the receiver taut against her ear. "I didn't mean it to go as far as this. I've been wrong. Give me the chance to tell him so . . . one day . . . "

As she waited tensely, during the constant buzzing at the other end of the line, she knew that whatever happened now, she would never be Clunes' wife. Truth and honesty of purpose had been slow in coming, but she recognised now that she had to find her own way back. The final challenge was between herself and Eugene. He had recognised this from the beginning, but she had not. She had been over slow in wakening to the truth, but having grasped it she would follow it to the end.

She glanced through the open window, down to the path below. A long shiver passed over her body. Part of her seemed to be already dying as she waited for the receiver to be lifted.

"I love Eugene. I love him."

The buzzing stopped, someone lifted the receiver.

"Eugene? Oh, thank God . . ."

"Where on earth are you? What's the matter?" His surprise heartened her and she tried to subdue her agitation in order to tell him where she was — and why.

"Have you got the address properly? I — I want to come back . . ."

He grasped the hurried explanations

instantly and did not argue.

"Don't you want me back?" she whispered despairingly.

"I'm coming for you." Displeasure sounded behind the curt words.

"You — you want me back, don't you?"

"Naturally I want you back. What's the matter with you? Wait there."

"I can't do anything else. I'm locked in. Hurry . . . hurry . . . " She replaced the receiver softly, and hurried towards the wash basin, where she began to wash her face and hands. I love Eugene, she thought dazedly.

Clunes entered the room presently, and seeing her engaged, he placed the glass he had brought on the dressing table. "I brought you a short drink."

"I didn't like you locking the door on me just now."

He pulled the towel away from her face, laughing at her expression.

"Promises made under duress have no value — or didn't you know?" He seemed in good humour and it was obvious that he had been regaling himself at the bar downstairs.

"I'm almost ready — and I'm really hungry. It's occurred to me that I haven't eaten all day. How will you like to have a starving female on your hands, Clunes?" She was afraid of him, and deliberately tried to lighten the tension between them so that he would not guess. If ever Clunes realised that she feared him her hold over him would have gone. What's the matter with me, she asked herself.

"I don't mind anything — so long as you are the female." He took her into his arms again, brushing his lips against her hair. "I love your hair, sweetheart . . . did you know? It always smells sweet — like warm hay."

"Really!" She pretended to an indignation she could not feel. It no longer mattered what he liked. Laughter was stiff on her lips as she fended him off. "I'm ready if you are."

Anything to get out of that prison. She must spin the meal out for hours if necessary. It would take Eugene an hour to reach them, even if he used the M.G. She pushed her hand under Clunes' arm in a companionable gesture.

"What an odd décor. I never care for those two colours together. Clunes, tell me about your next broadcast. When is it? I want to know everything." If she could keep him talking about his own affairs it would help the time along. She would not try to imagine what might happen when Eugene arrived. Oh, I'm hateful. What's the matter with me? She turned from the thought deliberately.

"Would you like me to serenade you, darling?" Clunes asked.

"Why not?"

"We have a balcony of sorts — but it seems to me I'd sooner be with you than climbing up the spouting." They reached the ground floor restaurant and found a table. Louella spent some time studying the menu. Clunes grew impatient and finally took it from her.

"You are like all women, don't know what you want to eat."

"You tell me then," she suggested.

"I will." He ordered their meal briskly, consulting the waiter. Presently he began to discuss his plans for the future and she was surprised to learn how far he had come already. Clunes was already in demand as a singer. He had an agent, and his future looked rosy.

"You certainly have the voice; we always knew that," she said.

His eyes thanked her. "If you have faith in me then I can keep going. I'll make it all up to you, Louella. I'll never let you be sorry that you threw in your lot with mine. I'll make life give you all you want . . . "

"We can't make life give us anything," she temporised. "We haven't any rights." She felt like a traitor as she listened, trying to say no word that would make her feel miserable later. Clunes was in a happy mood, and she began to feel more assured that all would come right. She deliberately loitered over the meal, searching her mind for questions with which to hold his interest.

"To say you were hungry, you haven't

eaten much," he was observant. "You're not enjoying any of this, are you?"

"Not really." To her surprise her eyes filled with tears and she sat back tragically, unable to conceal her dismay.

Clunes looked uncomfortable, glancing about him to see if her breakdown had been noticed. " Cheer up — we can go now if you're ready."

"I — I'll finish this." She looked at the iced pudding with growing distaste. Suddenly, through the open door, she heard Eugene's strong charming voice, enquiring for her at the reception. She knew she was safe. She leaned back again, staring at Clunes with frightened eyes.

"What the . . . who . . . that's Eugene?" Clunes glanced towards the door. "You?"

She clutched her bag in her hand and got to her feet, and fled. If there had to be a scene it had better not be in the crowded dining room. She ran straight to Eugene who was standing by the desk, hatless, unsmiling.

"Well?" There was sheer animosity in

his face and voice.

"What the hell are you doing here?" Clunes looked murderous as he followed Louella.

"I dropped in to pick up my wife. Any objections?" Eugene's coldness held a rapier quality, an antagonism that was as deadly as Clunes' more impetuous words. Louella stood near, trembling for the outcome. If only they could get away without a scene. She caught the eyes of the girl behind the desk and looked away quickly.

"I'm coming, Eugene."

"You're staying with me," Clunes took her wrist in his hand.

"She's coming with me, and if you interfere in any way, I'll hand you over to the police."

Clunes thrust his hands into his pockets. "Blast you . . . "

An odd look crossed Eugene's cold face. "I'd a feeling that might make you take your hands off her."

"What do you mean?" Clunes spoke sharply. "Damn you, what do you mean?"

Eugene shrugged contemptuously. "Get your things, Louella and join me here at once." She sped off to do his bidding, leaving them to quarrel or argue as they would.

"If you interfere with my wife again I'll put you on a charge — is that clear?" Eugene said stiffly.

"You don't suppose I kidnapped her, do you?" Clunes sneered.

"I'm not interested. What you do is your affair — this is mine. Now get out of my way, will you?" He saw Louella coming towards them and went to relieve her of the small suitcase she carried. "This all?"

"You're not really going?" Clunes' face was flushed, and be seemed unable to appreciate what was happening. There was a hesitation in him that made her feel a sudden deep pity for him. She should not have allowed matters to get so far out of hand.

"Yes, I'm going, Clunes. I'm sorry it's this way. I telephoned to Eugene and asked him to fetch me back. You'll realise later that it's better this way. Truly it is."

"You're going back to him?"

"I don't know what will happen."

Clunes turned his back on them, his clenched hands in his pockets for safety. He was a burly man, deeply passionate, uncomplicated, and Louella knew she was to blame for what was happening now. She followed Eugene to the waiting sports car. He drove back to London in complete silence, while she tried in vain to master her mounting terror.

Out of that silence he said briefly: "Why did you telephone for me?"

"I was frightened."

"You panicked — why?"

"I don't know. It all seemed wrong. Thank God you were home."

He did not probe further and presently they entered the house. Instantly they were plunged back into their worlds. Camille wakened to tears because she had not seen her father before he left the house again. Eugene rushed up to comfort his daughter, and when she learned that

Louella was back too, Louella had to hold her hand until she fell asleep again.

Almost at once the telephone rang, with a message from Claribel. Her date for flying the Atlantic had been brought nearer.

"I'm going on the fourth, darling," Claribel trilled. "What a rush to be ready in time. Would they allow me to take the sewing machine along too, do you think?"

Louella tried to be interested in Claribel's affairs, but she felt distracted by the conflicting calls on her time and patience. "If you have to go then the earlier date is better, because you'll be back so much sooner. Call me again in the morning, Claribel. We've only just got in and . . . "

"Anything wrong? You sound as depressed as cold soup. Oh, all right, I'll call you tomorrow. Goodnight." Claribel's gay voice ceased, and Louella turned back to find Eugene watching her.

"I know you're tired, Louella, but I'm afraid what I have to say won't wait for morning. I've been opening my mail — and had two telephone calls . . . you'd better come in here where we can discuss things. My lawyer has been up north to see your brother . . . "

"Wain? Is something wrong?" She followed him into his den.

"Your brother was released today — he's on his way with my lawyer and they may arrive tonight."

She shielded her eyes nervously. "Is he — free?"

"Yes. Wain is innocent."

She sat down, the strength leaving her limbs. Coming at the end of the day's disasters it was almost too much.

Eugene saw her distress and turned to consult the letters again. He picked one up in silence, read it through, before turning back to her. "Yes. Wain is innocent as you always believed him to be. It has been proved beyond any shadow of doubting."

"How?" she whispered.

He hesitated before revealing what the lawyer had said on the telephone a few minutes before. "They know who did the crime — it may not be murder, but almost certainly a verdict of manslaughter will be brought against . . . " he hesitated again. "This is going to be a shock to you, Louella — in several ways. They were picking Clunes up tonight. He will be charged with assault . . . robbery . . . "

She saw him through a muffling curtain of dark cloth. "Not Clunes. He was so sure that Wain was guilty. It couldn't be Clunes . . . he was so sure . . . so very sure . . . "

6

LOUELLA was lying in her own room, recovering from the faint. Eugene and Camille's nurse, were standing near, watching her. She sat up shuddering as memory returned.

"Are you feeling better now?" The nurse asked. She placed a glass on the side table, and put the stopper in a bottle she held.

"Sal volatile?" Louella asked. "Did I faint? I've never done that before. Odd."

Nurse prepared to leave the room. "If I'm needed I'll come down again but I think you'll be all right now."

Eugene was looking through the window, his back stiff, his manner repressive. "It was the shock of knowing about Clunes, wasn't it?"

"I suppose so. I might have been with him when they arrested him. How terrible that would have been."

He turned to watch her, as she sat on the side of the bed miserably.

"Why did you ring for me to bring you home, Louella?"

"I couldn't think of anyone else who could get there in time." She felt ashamed and weak. "If you hadn't been at home I'd have rung for the hotel manager — but it would have been pretty awful . . . "

"Then you intended to get away from Clunes?"

"Yes. I wanted to turn back on the way down but he wouldn't hear of it."

"No man worth his salt would have let you change your mind so late in the day. Don't you think you owe me more explanation than that?"

"Yes, I do . . . I realised while I was waiting on the line that I didn't love Clunes. That was why I left home — not those other reasons. I dare not tell him then . . . oh, who's this?"

Claribel knocked and entered the bedroom. She smiled at Eugene. "Thanks for ringing me. I was glad to come. What happened, Louella? I always thought you were as strong as an ox."

Having Claribel with her, helped Louella, and she was deeply grateful to Eugene for making it possible. Eagerly she poured out the story to her friend, when he left them to talk.

"He's not a bad type really," Claribel nodded at the closed door. "Has he wiped the floor with you — or is that in abeyance?"

"We haven't said much yet. He's annoyed . . . isn't he?"

"Would you expect less?" Claribel asked dryly. "Really, honey, you have been hasty. Why did you let Clunes persuade you?"

"If I knew the answer to that it would solve everything," Louella sighed. "If I'd known about Clunes before . . . "

"No one did — except Clunes. I wonder what's happened to him?"

"It's worse because he meant to let Wain take the blame. Oh, isn't it an awful mix up?" Louella shivered with shock.

"Why not have a meal? I could do with something too."

"Yes, let's go down and see what there is." Action was helpful and they left the room together, Claribel switching off the lights. "There will be something in the refrigerator." The two girls prepared a meal and presently asked Eugene to join them.

He was coming from his den to eat with them, when the doorbell rang, and he stayed to answer it. They listened intently, and suddenly Louella's pale face brightened.

"It's Wain. Eugene said he might arrive tonight. Oh . . . " She hurried from the room, straight into her brother's arms. "Oh, Wain . . . " She was so glad to see him, unable to believe that he was free again. She dug her fingers into his wide shoulders, laughing and crying together.

"Steady on," he warned. "This is the only good suit I've got." His spirits were high for he was laughing immoderately, too, and had just turned from shaking hands with Eugene, who watched the scene quietly.

Claribel who prided herself on her complete lack of sentimentality, was sniffing audibly. "Wain — you old so and so. I'm glad too."

The lawyer, who had accompanied Wain, stood in the background and for some minutes the conversation was general, before he declined their invitation to dine with them, and left the house.

Wain stood with one arm round Louella's waist. In spite of his high spirits there was a new gravity upon him, and gone forever was the boyishness which had been his until now. They continued to talk until Louella remembered the waiting meal.

"Let's all have something to eat — shall we?" She could not meet Eugene's glance as she led the way. For an hour they discussed the events that had led to this reunion.

"I saw father for a few minutes — it would have been longer only the train was due to pull out. He saw me off; he understood. I didn't want to go home for a while, but I will before I sail."

306

Louella looked at him. "Why? Where are you going, Wain?"

"Canada. The land of opportunity. I've always wanted to go, and the lawyer johnny told me that Eugene was paying for my ticket — flying. I think that's a pretty decent gesture under the circumstances."

"Hear, hear," Claribel murmured, glancing at their silent host. "Of course you are innocent, which helps a lot. If you really mean to go then this is it."

"Yes, I want to go. I'm grateful, Gene." The words came sincerely.

"That's all right," Eugene waved the words away.

"Soon?" Claribel hazarded.

"Everything is happening at once," Louella said. Their lives would go on in spite of what had happened. What happened to Clunes was something over which they had no control. He had placed himself outside their help. She thought about him with a sinking heart. Poor Clunes. "I'll take the tray away — if you've all quite finished."

She gathered up the plates and placed

them on the tray. Eugene rose to open the door for her, and switched on the hall light so that she could see her way. She paused at the kitchen door, balancing the tray on her hip while she switched on the light there.

Absently she placed the tray on the table, and was turning to the sink when she saw Clunes. He must have entered the house by the back door. There had been no sound. She stared at him, shocked into silence. His appearance was wild, his face dirty where he had evidently fallen, and his hair was rough.

Louella could not move from her position. This was some nightmare. In a moment she'd waken and scream, and someone would tell her not to be so silly, because such things didn't happen in real life.

Clunes watched her. She heard his rapid breathing. She heard the kitchen clock ticking loudly, the sounds of distant traffic. All was intensified in the nearer silence. This would not be the shock to Clunes that it was to her, for he had been seeking her, and fate had played into his hands.

"Clunes . . . " she whispered.

He moved swiftly between her and the door into the hall. "So — we meet again, Louella."

The words repelled and frightened her. Did he know that Wain was here? She must not scream for Wain would come, and Clunes would kill him. She stared in fear at Clunes' white face.

"You changed your mind," he said softly. "You were there, with me — and you double-crossed me. I don't forgive that in any woman — not even you, Louella."

She felt as if a cloud obscured part of her vision. "Are you . . . ?"

"You thought I was cooling off safely somewhere, didn't you? No, not Clunes. They'll never get me . . . or hold me. I knew the police meant to pick me up tonight, but I saw them first. They missed me in the darkness."

So he was a fugitive from justice? "You let me think . . . you let everyone believe

309

that it was Wain . . . why did you?"

"It was too easy, when he went the same evening. Who am I to quarrel with my luck?"

"Was it that? I believe something in me changed when you said you believed Wain guilty."

"That was my mistake," he admitted slowly. "I should have agreed with you. I didn't think you'd have taken it so hard. You're coming with me now, eh?"

She backed away from him. "I — can't. I don't love you. It isn't possible."

"I'm not leaving without you." The tone was no stronger than the previous one but it carried particular emphasis.

To gain time she whispered: "Where are you going?"

"Where no one will find us. I'm not going without you — that's for sure. If you evade me again I'll kill you . . . "

"Where would that get you?" she asked dryly. In their relationship there had ever been this dominating quality, and she realised the part it had played in her life. He had been the leader until she found the strength to break away and use her intelligence. "Clunes — listen to me . . . "

He turned to the door, for someone had entered the hall. In that moment of withdrawnness Louella rushed to the back door, flung it open, and shrieking at the top of her voice rushed headlong into the night.

The shadow that followed her was scarcely less swift, but she evaded his groping hands, and ran as she had not run since she was at school. She gained the silent back street and raced along its length. Clunes pounded after her, no longer intent on escaping, merely in silencing her for as she ran she continued to scream.

She gained the brighter lights of a main road, turned in to it thankfully, saw the gathering crowd, for help was coming from several directions at once. She sank down, breathing painfully, while Clunes passed her, turning in a lightning movement to evade the crowd.

"He's running towards the river." The

shout reached her as she tried to raise herself. She was sobbing spasmodically, crouching against a wall. Clunes was sllhouetted against the light of a street lamp, before he appeared to leap forward into the shadows.

Louella covered her face. It was here that Claribel found her.

"There, let me help you." Claribel's gentle voice was the only familiar sound in the nightmare in which she moved. "Come — before they all return. I'll help you. It's raining . . . "

"Where are Wain and Eugene?" She wanted to know if they were safe from Clunes but could not ask.

"They're hunting for Clunes. The police are here, too, so don't worry. They'll get him in time. He's quite a lad — your Clunes, isn't he?" Claribel talked as she guided her friend back to the house, which they entered through the front door. "We heard you scream, just after Eugene went to look for you. We thought you must be staying to wash up. There, feeling better now? Tell me what happened?" Claribel's curiosity got the better of discretion and she listened avidly as Louella tried to describe what had happened.

"He must have escaped the police escort, and came to find me. He wanted me to go with him. I'll go upstairs now, Claribel, do you mind? I can't bear any more tonight." She was crying quietly to herself as she dragged her feet up the wide stairs.

Presently she heard the men return, and Claribel came up to tell her there were detectives downstairs too. Louella sat shivering, too tired to undress, waiting in that deep void for news that might release her from her nightmare. Claribel stayed with her until Eugene entered. Louella was crying softly, pitifully, holding Claribel's hand.

"I'll stay for a while — thanks, Claribel," he said, holding the door for her to pass through. "If you'd stay the night it would help."

"All right — I will." She went along to the guest room thoughtfully. Just where did they all go from here?

"The police have left," Eugene said to Louella, when he had closed the door. "We've managed to piece it all together, but your evidence will be needed later." His voice was soothing, and she listened, trying to stop the hopeless crying.

"Thank you."

"Wain is sleeping on the couch tonight in my study. Do you want him?"

"No. Is he all right?"

"Yes. He sends you his love and says to keep your chin up."

She smiled, comforted by the message. "What happened — when you followed Clunes? I just saw him jump and that was all. Were you hurt?"

"No. We never got our hands on him; he had too good a start. Shall we leave it tonight? You are worn out."

"I'd rather know."

"Clunes jumped over the parapet into the river, and must have been stunned instantly against the stonework. They found his body . . . "

She looked down at her clasped hands

314

apathetically. "He said they'd not take him again. Oh, what shall I do? I feel to be so much to blame. If I hadn't been so easily persuaded, at least he wouldn't have come here tonight and he might have been alive now . . . "

"Did he wish you to go with him?"

"Yes. He hadn't forgiven me for changing my mind. Oh, I'm in a mess, aren't I?" Tears were running down her face again. Clunes was dear and she might never tell him now just how sorry she was for her part in the affair.

It was after midnight, and the sounds outside were muted. Eugene sat near her, one leg crossed over the other, not even smoking. He looked thoughtful. Louella looked at him, wondering of what he was thinking. Was he condemning her? Clunes would never see another day. His life was spent. Whatever he had done they had been friends in the past. The best in Clunes had been very fine. His mistakes had been more vital than some that were made. Her head ached so much that she could only think disjointedly.

"Why did you telephone me from the hotel earlier?" Eugene said as if the question was still unanswered in his mind. "You said you realised that you didn't love Clunes. Wasn't there more to it?"

"Wasn't that enough?" she asked faintly.

"Not for me — for us. I need a straight answer now, Louella. Did you suspect that he might be guilty of the crime for which Wain was taking the blame?"

"No. It never occurred to me."

"Yet you distrusted him?"

"I suppose so — yes. Subconsciously perhaps. I know now that it was all over between us before I left the north. One can be wise after the event. I'm not proud of myself, Eugene."

"Is it possible that you care for anyone else?"

"I don't know."

"Tonight we have to be honest with each other. After all that has happened we don't want to make any more mistakes. I want us to live together as man and wife, and we could if you shared my feeling. Is

316

it possible that you do? I'm not willing to continue as we are — is that clear?"

She raised her dark head defiantly. "You can't issue ultimatums. I'll never be your wife, while that woman remains in your life. What do you think I am? I wonder you dare talk this way to me."

He looked abashed. "Almira Ashton? But you know about her . . . "

"I do indeed. Have you seen the evening papers — when was it? So much has happened . . . " She was confused by the smile that was growing in his eyes.

"I believe you are jealous."

"Isn't there just cause?"

His attention was riveted on her. "You really mean that, don't you? Have we been at cross purposes the whole time?"

"I wouldn't know."

"Almira Ashton is not my mistress, if that's in your mind, Louella. I give you my word on that. I married you so that it never could be true. I've not the slightest intention of marrying her either. I have known Almira too long to trust my whole future in her small hands."

"But you said . . . "

"I said she bewitched and beguiled and tempted me — that is true. Any man would feel the way I do. She can be very — enchanting. She is a wonderful actress."

"Oh?" This was a new presentation of the facts as she knew them. The stories that went round the town had no foundation in fact. Eugene would not lie to her. Almira had wanted those stories to be true but she had not won him as she had hoped. Was it because his conquest was incomplete that their association had lasted?

"No, Louella, you'll have to think of a stronger reason than that. The evening I met you, I wanted to know you better. You surprised me by your bitter, worldly attitude, and for a while I was puzzled. I didn't get your measure. It was only later that I realised I could have been mistaken, and that you were not what you seemed, when you agreed to my terms . . . "

Her gaze was fixed on the carpet and she was unable to look up.

He leaned nearer, and his tone held a coaxing note. "What right had you to be jealous, anyway?"

She blushed vividly, feeling eclipsed. Eugene came nearer and kissed her. It was a gentle, seeking kiss, a kiss of forgiveness.

"Seeing you don't care for the other chap, would there be a chance for me?" he whispered, against her mouth.

"There — might." They were both smiling.

"I liked you from our first meeting. But you sounded so hard headed. You knew what you wanted all right, and I decided to give you a run for your money. I'd no intention of letting you escape me, Louella."

"Yet everything has gone wrong . . . " she mourned.

"Not everything. When you put this sadness away you'll see that everything is right . . . if you love me."

"Yes." She spoke thoughtfully. "It took

me a long time to realise that I do love you. If I could have set you against Clunes without anything in the way to clutter my vision, I'd have chosen you. Now I know . . . "

"Almira doesn't count?"

"Not any more."

He was laughing tenderly. "Poor Almira. She'll have to be content with her Ramon. He's a nice chap and she'll settle down in time." He was drawing her to him. "How does it feel to be in the clear at last, darling?"

She could not meet the look in his eyes. "Rather wonderful."

"So — we return to Gotland?" he said. "You never thought we would, did you?"

"I had not your faith." They were silent, remembering those days and nights of magic on the scented island. Moonlight on the glittering water, the whispering silences, the feeling of familiarity with their surroundings. She had tried to remain faithful to the past, yet weren't past and present and future inextricably bound within the framework of one's own personality? It was a sobering thought.

Eugene watched her, content in the moment. She turned to him, understanding at last.

"Always remember I love you, Gene."

Dawn was sweeping darkness from the sky, London was awakening to a new day, the subdued, hesitant sounds came distinctly to their ears.

"Another day . . . " Eugene said, and he was smiling.

THE END

CRUSADING NURSE
Jane Converse

It was handsome Dr. Corbett who opened Nurse Susan Leighton's eyes and who set her off on a lonely crusade against some powerful enemies and a shattering struggle against the man she loved.

WILD ENCHANTMENT
Christina Green

Rowan's agreeable new boss had a dream of creating a famous perfume using her precious Silverstar, but Rowan's plans were very different.

DESERT ROMANCE
Irene Ord

Sally agrees to take her sister Pam's place as La Chartreuse the dancer, but she finds out there is more to it than dyeing her hair red and looking like her sister.

HEART OF ICE
Marie Sidney

How was January to know that not only would the warmth of the Swiss people thaw out her frozen heart, but that she too would play her part in helping someone to live again?

LUCKY IN LOVE
Margaret Wood

Companion-secretary to wealthy gambler Laura Duxford, who lived in Monaco, seemed to Melanie a fabulous job. Especially as Melanie had already lost her heart to Laura's son, Julian.

NURSE TO PRINCESS JASMINE
Lilian Woodward

Nick's surgeon brother, Tom, performs an operation on an Arabian princess, and she invites Tom, Nick and his fiancé to Omander, where a web of deceit and intrigue closes about them.

THE WAYWARD HEART
Eileen Barry

Disaster-prone Katherine's nickname was "Kate Calamity", but her boss went too far with an outrageous proposal, which because of her latest disaster, she could not refuse.

FOUR WEEKS IN WINTER
Jane Donnelly

Tessa wasn't looking forward to meeting Paul Mellor again — she had made a fool of herself over him once before. But was Orme Jared's solution to her problem likely to be the right one?

SURGERY BY THE SEA
Sheila Douglas

Medical student Meg hadn't really wanted to go and work with a G.P. on the Welsh coast although the job had its compensations. But Owen Roberts was certainly not one of them!

HEAVEN IS HIGH
Anne Hampson

The new heir to the Manor of Marbeck had been found. But it was rather unfortunate that when he arrived unexpectedly he found an uninvited guest, complete with stetson and high boots.

LOVE WILL COME
Sarah Devon

June Baker's boss was not really her idea of her ideal man, but when she went from third typist to boss's secretary overnight she began to change her mind.

ESCAPE TO ROMANCE
Kay Winchester

Oliver and Jean first met on Swale Island. They were both trying to begin their lives afresh, but neither had bargained for complications from the past.

CASTLE IN THE SUN
Cora Mayne

Emma's invalid sister, Kym, needed a warm climate, and Emma jumped at the chance of a job on a Mediterranean island. But Emma soon finds that intrigues and hazards lurk on the sunlit isle.

BEWARE OF LOVE
Kay Winchester

Carol Brampton resumes her nursing career when her family is killed in a car accident. With Dr. Patrick Farrell she begins to pick up the pieces of her life, but is bitterly hurt when insinuations are made about her to Patrick.

DARLING REBEL
Sarah Devon

When Jason Farradale's secretary met with an accident, her glamorous stand-in was quite unable to deal with one problem in particular.

ROMANTIC LEGACY
Cora Mayne

As kennelmaid to the Armstrongs, Ann Brown, had no idea that she would become the central figure in a web of mystery and intrigue.

THE RELENTLESS TIDE
Jill Murray

Steve Palmer shared Nurse Marie Blane's love of the sea and small boats. Marie's other passion was her step-brother. But when danger threatened who should she turn to — her step-brother or the man who stirred emotions in her heart?

ROMANCE IN NORWAY
Cora Mayne

Nancy Crawford hopes that her visit to Norway will help her to start life again. She certainly finds many surprises there, including unexpected happiness.

UNLOCK MY HEART
Honor Vincent

When Ruth Linton, a young widow with three children, inherits a house in the country, it seems to be the answer to her dreams. But Ruth's problems were only just beginning . . .

SWEET PROMISE
Janet Dailey

Erica had met Rafael in Mexico, where their relationship had been brief but dramatic. Now, over a year later in Texas, she had met him again — and he had the power to wreck her life.

SAFARI ENCOUNTER
Rosemary Carter

Jenny had to accept that she couldn't run her father's game park alone; so she let forceful Joshua Adams virtually take over. But Joshua took over her heart as well!

When
interv
was f
assign
repair
his ex-

"A bori
morals,
Demajo
about t
is Maria

STARS

Secretly
Doordni
been thr
marry hi
for pract

NEATH PORT TALBOT LIBRARY
AND INFORMATION SERVICES

1 10/04	25	49	73
2	26	50	74
3	27 8/07	51	75
4	28	52 9/08	76
5 10/13	29	53	77
6 3/13	30	54	78
7 5/03	31	55	79
8	32	56	80
9	33 1/07	57	81
10 8/05	34	58 11/12	82
11	35	59	83
12	36	60	84
13	37	61	85
14	38 7/08	62 9/15	86
15 5/09	39	63	87
16	40	64	88
17 5/08	41	65	89
18	42	66	90 7/12
19	43	67	91
20	44 6/06	68 11/14	92
21	45	69	COMMUNITY SERVICES
22	46	70	
23	47	71	
24 4/12	48	72	NPT/111